For Greater Things:
The story of
Saint Stanislaus Kostka

William T. Kane

Contents

FOR GREATER THINGS:
THE STORY OF
SAINT STANISLAUS KOSTKA

BY

William T. Kane

PREFACE

Among Christian evidences the heroic virtue and holiness of Catholic youth must not be overlooked. Juvenile and adolescent victories of a conspicuous kind, over the flesh, the world, and the devil, can be found in no land and in no age, except a Christian land and age, and in no Church except the Catholic Church. It is of all excellences the very rarest and most difficult, this triumphant mastery over human weakness and human pride. It has defied the life-long strivings of men whom the world recognizes as beings of superior wisdom and power of will. The philosophers who have described it most beautifully and encouraged its pursuit in the most glowing and impressive terms remain themselves sad examples of human futility in the struggle to disengage the spirit from the claws of dragging and unclean influences. For the forces of evil are infinite in their variety, insidious beyond the ability of natural sharpness to detect and guard against, and unsleeping in the pressure of their siege upon the heart of man. Who will explain how it comes to pass that youth, whose callowness and inexperience are the mockery of the world, has laid prostrate in single combat this giant of evil and won fields where the reputations of the world's wisest and noblest and most tried lie buried?

It is a matter of idle curiosity with us how an unbelieving generation, ingenious in devising natural explanations (which are most unnatural) of supernatural phenomena, would explain away the wonder of the young Saint's life which is the subject of the following pages. It presents to us a picture of Divine Condescension guiding and inspiring and aiding human effort, so convincingly clear and transparent in its smallest details and in its general effect as to seem outside the pale of all possible mutilation and misinterpretation by malice or skeptical analysis. Natural reaction against sinful excess, thwarted ambitions, disappointed hopes, meek conformity with environment, ecclesiastical manipulation of pliant material, tame acquiescence in family traditions and arrangements, these and all the other stock "explanations," with which a groveling world seeks to pull down the Saints to its own dreary level, cannot be invoked to dissipate the mystery and the glory surrounding Stanislaus. How did he come so early in life, and in a nobleman's family, to set such store upon spiritual values? How did his tender and immature mind grasp with such swift sureness the one lesson of all philosophies, that life on its material side is an incident rather than the sum of human existence and can never satisfy the soul's desires ? How could this mere boy have developed, so young, an iron will which wrought that hardest of all laborious tasks, namely, the conformation of conduct with lofty ideals? There are supernatural answers to these and similar questions which might be raised concerning the brief career of St. Stanislaus. We know of no merely natural answers.

The lively and energetic style adopted in the present biography may create a trace of mild surprise in older readers. Sanctity, it is true, some one may say, is a very beautiful achievement in a world of poor and, at best, mediocre performance; but, after all, the business of sanctity is a serious business. It calls for grit and endurance, and, as a picture, is only saved from the sordid by spiritual motives which are unseen. If all moral life is a monotonous warfare, the life of a Saint is warfare in the very first ranks where the trenches are filled with water and the shells fall thickest and the general discomfort and pettiness are at their maximum. It is misleading and not in strict accord with known realities, to paint the portrait of a Saint in rose color and sunlight, diffusing an iridescent atmosphere of cheerful gayety and buoyancy.

The criticism is not without some foundation; but youthful readers will not adopt it. For youth is generous, and age is crabbed. And because Saints never become crabbed we are right in concluding that they always remain youthful. And, to draw out our conclusion, the lives of Saints, contrary to the popular belief, are much more interesting to the child than they are to the man. It is a pity that Catholic parents do not recognize this outstanding truth. No Saint's life is dull to the average intelligent child. Grown-ups are dull: they never yield to sublime impulses: they measure, calculate, practice a hard-and-fast moderation, reduce the splendid possibilities of life to a drab level of safe actuality, and pursue ideals at a canny and cautious pace. Not so the Saints. They always retained the freshness and confidence and generous impulses of childhood. If God spoke to their inner ear and bade them leap boldly forth into His Infinite Arms, spurning irretrievably the solid footing of our spinning globe, without hesitation or question they took the leap. And every child can see the wisdom of it. To the child it is common sense: to his elders it is inspired heroism or unintelligible hardihood. We have always entertained a deep-seated suspicion that there is no child who does not think it easy to be a Saint, so native is sanctity to Catholic childhood. Cardinal Newman, we believe, exhorted us all to make our sacrifices for God while we are young before the calculating selfishness of old age gets hold of us.

Still it may not be quite clear to the inquiring mind why the desperate difficulties of sainthood can be truthfully viewed in the light of a breathless adventure. Learn, then, the great secret. The love of God in the heart is the magical light which touches the dreariness and hardship of self-thwarting with a splendor of sublime Romance. You cannot have holiness without love. Holiness can be either greater nor less than the love of God. Let this love faint or grow cold, there is at once a loss of holiness, even though it retain all its external gear. This is a cardinal truth; it is a key which will solve many a puzzle. It will explain why fanatics and similar oddities are not Saints, though secular history sometimes honors them with the title.

Merely concede that the Saint possesses love for God in an extraordinary measure and degree, and it is the most comprehensible thing in the world that he will not only accept all tests of his love readily, but will go forth in search of them with eager alacrity. First and last and always the only keen satisfaction of great love, whether human or divine, is to welcome opportunities of proving itself in some heroic form of courage and endurance. Danger, suffering, battling against odds, discouragement, overwork, pain of mind and body, failure, want of recognition, rebuffs, contempt and persecution, are no longer the subject matter of a strong-jawed stoicism or a submissive patience but rather the quickening bread and wine of an intense and high-keyed life. This is why the Saints, be the provocation ever so great, never develop nerves, or experience those melancholy and humiliating reactions which are the natural ebb-tide of spiritual energies. This is why Saints can fast and keep their temper sweet, can wear hair-shirts without cultivating wry faces, can be passed by in the distribution of honors without being soured, can pray all night without robbing the day of its due meed of cheerfulness, can rise superior to frailties and weaknesses without despising those who cannot, can be serious without being testy and morose, can live for years in a cell or a desert or a convent-close without perishing of ennui or being devoured by restlessness, and can mingle with life, where all its currents meet, without losing their heads or swerving a hairbreadth from the straight line of a most uncommon and most impressive kind of common sense.

Unless we keep before our eyes this mainspring of a Saint's life, that life will be as enigmatical to us as it is to the world. Jesus balked at no test of the love which He bore towards us: nay, He devised tests passing all human imagining. Let Him make trial of our love for Him! We are unhappy till He does! And with this daring spirit in his heart every Saint enters upon a career of Romance in its sweetest and highest form. And, we submit, to recur to the literary style of the following biography, Romance is light-hearted, light-stepping, cheerful, with the starlight on its face and in its eyes.

James J. Daly, S.J.

CHAPTER I
ON THE ROAD

Mid-August in Vienna, the year 1567: when Shakespeare was still a little boy; twenty years before Philip II fitted out the Spanish Armada; forty years before the first English colony settled in America. The sun had just well risen, the gates of Vienna had been opened but a few hours. Through the great western gate, which cast its long shadow on the road to Augsburg, came a strange-looking boy.

He lacked but a month or two of seventeen years, was some five feet two or three inches in height, had an oval face of remarkable beauty and liveliness, jet black hair, and eyes in which merriment dwelt as in its home. He was dressed as became a noble of the time, and in apparel of unusual splendor and costliness; plumed bonnet, slashed velvet doublet, tight silken hose, jeweled dagger at his girdle.

But it was odd to see so brilliant a figure on foot in the dusty highway; still more odd that be carried a rough bundle slung on a staff over his and that, peasant fashion, he munched at a loaf of bread as he trudged the road.

By no means stalwart-looking, still he swung along with an easy stride and a confident strength that many a stouter man might envy. He was bound for Augsburg, 400 miles to the west, and he set himself thirty miles a day as his rate of travel.

He wore splendid clothes, because he was Stanislaus, the son of John Kostka, Lord of Kostkov, Senator, and Castellan of Zakroczym in the Duchy of Mazovia, Poland. He ate his rough breakfast, like a peasant, on the road, because he had just been to Mass and received Holy Communion at the Jesuit church in Vienna. He carried a bundle on his staff, because he laughed merrily at fine clothes and had in the bundle a coarse tunic and a stout pair of brogans, which he meant to put on as soon as he got well out of the city. And his face and his eyes shone with joy, because he loved God most wonderfully and was as happy a boy as ever moved through this dull world.

Every age has its adventurers: men who for fame, or for place, or for money, cross wide seas, fight brave battles, endure great hardships. The age in which Stanislaus lived was filled with them. All the world reads with delight the story of such men. And every decent boy who reads feels himself, if only for the moment, their fellow in spirit, eager to do what they did and as bravely as they did.

But was there ever adventure finer than this, ever spirit more gayly daring? Stanislaus Kostka, son of a noble house, a boy in years, starting without a copper in his pocket to cross half of Europe afoot! And for what? Not to have men say what a brave chap he was; not to win a name, or rank, or money: but because God would be pleased by his doing it, because God called him to do something which he could not do in Vienna.

He felt he had a vocation to be a Jesuit. He knew his father would not consent. He took six months to think it over, to pray for light, to make sure it was no mere whim or fancy of his own, but the very voice of God. And when he felt sure, he left a letter for his brother Paul and his tutor, Bilinski, with whom he had been studying in Vienna; he gave his money to a couple of beggars; he said, "If God wants me to do this, He'll furnish the means"; he put on his best attire, tied up a rough suit in a cloth, took a stout staff in his hand, and with God's blessing upon him and His Eucharistic Presence in his heart, stepped out cheerfully on a journey that would stagger most men.

That is the stuff of which heroes are made. If Stanislaus had done this for the glory of the world, we should have his praises in our histories, we should have stories woven about him, the whole world would cry "Bravo!" But he did it for God, and the world cannot understand him at all: the world is silent.

An hour or so of that steady, tireless stride carried him well away from Vienna. He slipped off his velvet and silk, put on his coarse tunic - a shirt-like garment that came below his knees - girded himself with a bit of rope, tied his stout shoes on his feet, and took the road again. There were folk aplenty journeying from the countryside to Vienna in the early morning. Stanislaus picked out one of the poorest-looking peasants and handed him the gala dress he had just taken off.

"I can't carry these with me, friend," he said. "Won't you please take them? I have no use for them, and perhaps you can sell them in the city."

And he was gone before the peasant, gaping in wonder at the rich garments and dagger in his hands, could much more than catch a glimpse of that bright face and those laughing eyes.

He tramped all day, and made his thirty miles. When he was hungry, he asked some one he met for food. It is not likely that any one would refuse the smiling, handsome boy, from whose face innocence simply shone. But if any one had refused him, it would not have annoyed Stanislaus. His good humor came from heaven, as well as from his own cheery soul - and you cannot rebuff that kind of good humor.

Night came down at last, and he was tired out. He came to an inn and asked for shelter.

"I have no money," he told the landlord, smiling, "and I have no claim upon you. Will you take me in?"

The landlord looked at him shrewdly a little, then said with respect:

"But what is your grace doing in such a garb?"

Stanislaus thought for a moment that he was recognized; but he put on a bold front, and laughed as he said:

"I am not 'your grace. I am what you see me, and I have a long journey to make."

In those days it was not unusual for even nobles to go, roughly clad, upon pilgrimages of devotion. That Stanislaus was a noble, the landlord was quite certain. That he might be engaged on some such pious business, was possible. But who ever heard of a mere boy going upon pilgrimage?

The whole affair puzzled the landlord more than a little. However, the face of the boy reassured him. At least there could be no evil behind that frank, brave countenance. So he shook his head, saying:

"I do not understand. But come in. You are welcome."

He gave Stanislaus his supper and a bed to sleep in.

"You shall not be the poorer for this," said Stanislaus, as he thanked him. "You know God makes it up to us for even a cup of cold water given in His name."

And as the boy spoke, the landlord saw his face glow when he spoke of God and he was very glad at heart that he had given shelter and food, to this strange boy.

Stanislaus slept soundly. But he was up with the sun, washed and dressed quickly, and went to thank his host again before setting out.

"But you will have something to eat before you go?" cried the man, as Stanislaus stood before him, staff in hand, ready for the road.

"It is good of you to offer it," the boy answered. "But perhaps I shall find a church before long, and I must go fasting to Holy Communion."

Then the landlord marvelled again, for at that period even good people did not go very often to Holy Communion, especially when they were traveling hard, as Stanislaus evidently was. And his admiration and liking grew for this boy with the merry face and the heart so near heaven.

"At least," he said, "you must take something with you for the way."

And that Stanislaus did not refuse, but accepted gratefully, and so parted from the kind landlord, leaving him gazing in the doorway with wonder in his eyes.

His legs were a bit stiff and sore this second day. But the first few miles wore that off, and he swung on his way as bravely and gayly as before.

CHAPTER II
THE PURSUIT

Meanwhile, there was a hubbub in Vienna. Stanislaus had lived in that city about three years with his brother Paul, who was about a year older than he, and in the care of a tutor, a young man named Bilinski. He had left them in the early morning. As the day wore on and he did not return home, they became uneasy. They went about all afternoon, inquiring amongst their friends and acquaintance if any had seen him. Only one or two were in the secret, and they kept discreet silence.

Unable therefore to get any trace of Stanislaus, they soon came to the conclusion that he had fled. And, as we shall see, they had good reason in their own hearts for guessing that from the first. They returned to the house of the Senator Kimberker, where they were all lodging, and taking Kimberker, who was a Lutheran, into their confidence, they held a council of war.

It was decided that Stanislaus must have gone to Augsburg. Paul recalled something that Stanislaus had said to him only the day before, when he had threatened plainly to run away. And they had heard him say, another time, that at Augsburg was Peter Canisius, the Provincial of the German Jesuits. Of course they were going to follow him and bring him back. But night had come on before their inquiries and deliberations were finished. They must wait till the next day.

Accordingly, bright and early the following morning, all three, with one of the Kostkas' servants, drove out in a carriage over the Augsburg road. They had four good horses and they told their coachman not to spare the whip. They came to the inn where Stanislaus had spent the night. They questioned the landlord.

"Have you seen a boy of seventeen, a Polish noble, pass westward along this road yesterday or today?"

But the landlord was shrewd, and though the whole matter was beyond him, he fancied somehow that these eager folk were no great friends of the boy who had lodged with him. And as he trusted that boy and could scarcely help being loyal to him, he shrugged his shoulders and answered:

"How should I know? So many travel this road."

Then Bilinski described Stanislaus and his doublet of velvet and hose of silk and jeweled dagger. But at that the landlord shook his head in denial.

"I have seen no such person as your graces describe," he said.

Bilinski called out to the coachman:

"Drive on. We have nothing to learn here."

But Paul said: "NO, let us turn back. He cannot have walked this far in one day. We must have passed him on the road."

"Perhaps you could not have walked so far," said Bilinski, with a sneer. "But Stanislaus could. Drive on!"

Forty miles or more out of Vienna, they saw a boy trudging ahead of them, in a rough tunic, rope-girdled, with a staff in his hand. At the noise of the hurrying wheels the boy glanced back, then quickly turned up a lane which there entered the road. He did not look in the least like a nobleman's son, and the carriage passed the bottom of the lane without so much as slacking speed.

Stanislaus ran up the lane until he came to where it ended at a rough, brawling stream. Without a moment's hesitation he put off his shoes, tucked up his tunic, and began wading in the course of the stream. The water was cold, the sharp stones in the bed of the stream bruised his feet, at any moment he might fall into a deep hole and be drowned. But he splashed and stumbled ahead, as fast as he could go, praying to his guardian angel to have care of him. A little farther, he knew, the highway crossed this stream by a bridge, and there he could leave the water and regain the road.

The carriage meantime kept on and came to this bridge. But Paul had been thinking of the young fellow who took to the lane when he saw the carriage approach and a shrewd suspicion came into his head.

"Did you see that boy who ran up the lane?" he cried at length to Bilinski. "I believe it was Stanislaus."

"But he was dressed like a peasant," said Bilinski. "And Stanislaus had on a handsome suit."

They debated for a time, but Paul prevailed. Round they turned and drove furiously back to the lane. But as the driver tried to turn his horses into it, the animals reared and balked and refused to enter. Blows and curses were showered on them; they merely stood and trembled; no efforts could urge them into the lane. Then the driver grew afraid, and cried out:

"My Lord Paul, we cannot go into this lane. And before God, I have fear upon me! Never have the horses acted this way."

And indeed fear seized them all. They saw the hand of God in this strange obstinancy of their beasts. Even Kimberker cried the pursuit.

"Fear God!" he said. "For this is no common mishap!"

And when they turned the horses' heads again toward Vienna, the animals snorted and pranced and went very willingly.

And so, when Stanislaus came to the bridge, the highway was clear. After a look about, he put on his shoes, gripped his staff afresh, and took up again cheerily as ever his thirty miles a day to Augsburg.

Day after day, tired and footsore, he told off the long miles, begging his food and lodging as he went; fearless and happy, praying like an angel of God as he walked along.

Many were kind to him for the brave, bright spirit that shone out in his face. Many remembered those words of our Lord, "Whatsoever you have done unto the least of these my brethren, you have done it unto me," and willingly sheltered the boy and gave him to eat. Sometimes he turned into the fields beside the road and slept through the warm August night beneath the open sky. Whenever he came to a church in the morning, he heard Mass and received Holy Communion, for he started out each morning fasting. And on the fourteenth day he reached Augsburg.

What happened there, we shall see in another chapter, and how within three weeks this smiling boy turned his face southward and tramped another eight hundred miles on foot to Rome. But just that will show you something of the spirit of Stanislaus, the spirit of a hero. All that a knight might do out of love for his lady, he did out of love for God. He really loved God with a sort of fierce intensity. And he wanted to show his love in deeds, just as we want to show our love for a person by doing something, by giving something. God had given him everything, he would give God everything: that was the whole of his life. And with that generosity went a fine common sense. He was not rash or headlong, acting first and thinking afterward. He reckoned things out calmly and sensibly, and then went ahead with a pluck and determination that nothing in the world could stop.

God asked a fearfully hard thing of him; to leave his people, his home; to set out afoot on an enormous journey; to undergo no end of hardships and humiliations; to live in a strange land, among strange people. And he did it, did it smilingly, joyfully, with a simple, quiet bravery seldom if ever matched by any other boy in the world.

The one thing that staggers us is his reason for doing it, his great love for God. And that is because we have not got, what we could easily get, his secret. He prayed, he kept close in thought to God always. God and heaven and our Lady were as familiar to his mind as the sun and the earth and the air are to our mind's. The earth to him was only the antechamber of heaven. He looked upon life as one looks upon a little delay at a railway station before the train leaves; the only important thing is to catch the train.

CHAPTER III
EARLY DAYS

Bilinski and Paul Kostka went back to Vienna, much troubled at heart. They really loved Stanislaus, for one thing, though they had been pretty rough with him. And for another, they had to face the anger of the Lord John Kostka, when he should hear of Stanislaus' flight.

Shortly after they had got back, a young friend of the runaway came to them and said:

"If you look between the leaves of such-and-such a book, you will find a letter which Stanislaus left for you."

They looked and found the letter. It was very simple and straightforward, a genuine boy's letter. He had run away, he said, because he had to. He was called to enter the Society of Jesus. He had to do what God wanted of him. He knew they would prevent him if they could. And so he just went. He left them messages of affectionate regard, and begged them to forward his letter to his father.

Bilinski sent this letter on at once. Paul also wrote, as did Kimberker and even the servant who had gone with them in the carriage. Each tried to shift the blame from himself, told of the strange behavior of the horses, explained that everything possible had been done to overtake the fugitive.

And when their letters came, there was high wrath in Kostkov. The Lord John raved and swore. He blamed everybody, but most of all Stanislaus and the tricky Jesuits who, he said, were back of the whole scheme. He wrote to Cardinal Osius that he would not rest until he had broken up the Jesuit college in Pultowa and driven every schemer of them out of Poland. As for Stanislaus, he would follow him across the world, if need were, and drag him back to Kostkov in chains.

He was a great lord, the Lord John. He loved his second son, Stanislaus, most dearly, and he loved dearly the honor of his house, which he thought that son had stained by hi& conduct. A son of his in beggar's garb, tramping the highways of Europe, begging his bread from door to door! It nearly broke his heart.

He had princely blood in his veins, he was a Senator of Poland, he might even become a king. His dearest hopes were in Stanislaus, his second son. Paul, the eldest, was wild and unsteady. And though there were two other sons and a daughter, none gave such promise as Stanislaus. So that the Lord John looked chiefly to him to carry on the great name and make it more glorious still. No wonder he raged!

Stanislaus had figured all that out beforehand. It hurt him too, hurt terribly. But what can one do when God calls? God had made all the Kostkas, given them name and rank. God was the Lord of Lords. It was heart-breaking to Stanislaus to leave his father in anger. Yet he trusted that since that was God's will - well, God would find a way to bring peace out of all this trouble. He put all his fears and heartache away from him, and went out to do what God wanted.

He had always done that, even when he was a little tad in the rough castle at Kostkov. God had taught him, God had helped him wonderfully. But more wonderful still to our eyes is the way the boy listened to God's teaching and obeyed it.

We think things come easy to the saints. We read or hear of wonders in their lives, which are evidently God's doing; and we say:

"Of course the saint was good and holy. But it was all done for him. God made everything smooth. The saint was never in my boots for a minute."

And all the time we forget the things which the saint himself did, the superb efforts he had to make.

So Stanislaus began to pray as soon as he well began to speak. Do you think he would not sooner have kept on with his play? Do you think he did not naturally hate the effort just as any boy naturally hates effort?

He lived amongst rough men, men used to the ways of camps and the speech of soldiers. Yet he not merely kept his own lips" clean, but he shrank, as from a blow, from every coarse or indecent speech in others. He did not go around correcting people. He was too sensible for that. He was not a prig or a prude. But he knew, as we know, that vile speech is hateful to God; and, as so many of us do not do, he set his face against it.

Did that cost him no effort? Had he no human respect to fight against? Think of how many times you may have grinned, cowardly, at a gross remark or shady story of a comrade - because you were not fighter enough to resent it! And then give this Stanislaus, who did resent, credit for his stouter courage, his more manly spirit.

His biographers tell us that he was simply' free from temptations against purity. That does not mean what many may think it means: that he was physically unlike other boys, that he had no animal desires, that he had nothing to fight against. It means that he was such a magnificent fighter that he had won the battle almost from the start. It means that he was not content, as so many of us are, with merely pushing a temptation a little aside, and then looking around in surprise to find it still there. He was like a skillful boxer, who wards off every blow of his adversary, so that he goes through the contest absolutely untouched. He watched, as we are too lazy to watch; he kept out of danger, where we foolishly run into it; he did not wait until temptation had set upon him and nearly battered him down before he began to resist; he saw it coming afar off, just as we can if we look out, and he met it with a rush that sent it again beyond reach or even sight.

OF COURSE he was the same as other boys; OF COURSE he had the same inclinations, the same promptings of the animal man; but with them he had more daring, more force and energy of will to cooperate with God's grace.

You always find it that way. The things the saints seem to do with ease are terrifically hard things, huge battles, regular slugging fights. The ease, if there be any, is not in the things they did, but in the men who did them.

You have seen skilled pianists sit down at their instruments and run off into brisk flowing music what looks like a hopeless jumble of notes. You may have seen an artist sketch in, whilst chatting idly, a swift, striking portrait. Well, all really good men are artists too; artists in fighting. And Stanislaus was one of the cleverest and strongest artists of the lot.

He began early, just as the musician Mozart did, just as the painter Raffaele did; and he studied hard at his art, just as all great artists have done. He began by saying his prayers well, not mere lip prayers, but heart prayers. He began by getting on easy terms with God, with our Lord in the Blessed Sacrament, with our Blessed Lady. He learned to talk with them as we learn to talk with our fathers and mothers. He told them his troubles, his plans. He talked everything over with them. And it no more made him queer or stiff or unpleasant than talking things over with your comrades or your parents makes you queer or stiff or unpleasant. If you believe in God, it is the most natural thing in the world to try to take Him into your confidence.

Then it is easy to see how, as Stanislaus grew older, he liked to pray, he liked to talk about God and our Lady. You see, he had grown to know them. They were not remote, far away. They were as near to him as his own folk. They were his own folk. And it is easy to see how, keeping in God's sight all the time, he kept his soul clean and his heart merry.

CHAPTER IV
OFF TO VIENNA

In this way Stanislaus went on until he was nearly fourteen years old and his brother Paul was approaching fifteen. Then the Lord John Kostka thought his boys had better continue their studies, not at home, but at a regular school. He picked out John Bilinski, a young man who had lately completed his college course, as tutor for them. He gave them a couple of servants, mounted them all on good horses, and sent them off six hundred miles or more on horseback to Vienna.

You may be sure Stanislaus enjoyed the long ride. It would be strange if he, a nobleman of the finest cavalry nation in the world, were not a good horseman. He loved the smell of the open fields, he loved the boisterous song of the mountain torrent. The hills and the plains were his home, for the hills and the plains were nearer to God than the houses of men.

In those days all travel was on foot or on horseback. The wealthy and noble rode, the poor footed it. Great highways cut Europe from end to end; though there were tracts in Stanislaus' country where the roadway was only the broad steppe, where the grasses waved and tossed like the sea, where men were few and their dwellings scattered far apart.

They crossed great rivers, they climbed the foothills of the Carpathian mountains. Many a night Paul and Stanislaus, with their people, slept under the stars. Many a wild, rough border town they passed. Many a great forest they penetrated, the home of the wild boar and the aurochs.

And the tar burners in the forests looked up from under their matted brows at the fair oval face of the Polish boy, and said:

"He is like a wild flower blown by the wind. He is like the violets that laugh in spring at the sun."

And the shaggy fighting-men of the frontier villages watched him ride through their streets, and thought:

"This is an angel. He looks toward heaven because he sees his Brothers there."

They crossed themselves piously as he passed. And some of the light and laughter of his face glowed 'for a moment in their dark lives, as a gloomy glen in the forest is brightened up by a darting ray of sunlight.

He was wonderful, but he was always a boy. He was glad to feel the good horse under him, to grip the Tartar saddle with his knees, to feel the air rush by his cheek.

Sometimes they met poor people staggering wearily afoot along the road. Often Stanislaus checked his horse and lightly dismounted.

"Get up, get up, old father!" he would cry. "My legs are stiff from the saddle. I want to walk."

And though a peasant might often be afraid to accept the favor from a noble, or be surly and churlish, the folk never were so with Stanislaus. Up climbed the old father into the saddle, and Stanislaus stepped out by his side.

"God give your grace long years!" said the thankful old man.

"Long years!" cried Stanislaus. I want more than that. I want eternity. I was born for greater things than long years."

And the old man would understand; for he was of the poor, and the poor know more of this longing for heaven than do the rich. But he looked almost with awe at this richly dressed noble boy who had learned even now to value life so justly. Then it was easy for Stanislaus to talk of heaven to the old man.

"Old father, in the barony of the Lord Jesus there is no poverty or old age or weariness. Nor is there any difference of rank there as here, for we shall all be great lords and castellans in heaven."

"Aye, but your grace will be a hetman surely in the army of the Lord Jesus," said the old man.

"Who knows!" cried Stanislaus. "I should love that dearly. Though the generals in His kingdom are not always from amongst the nobles. It may be that you will be hetman, and I a common soldier. But it is good to be even a common soldier with

Him."

"I went against the Tartars in my youth," said the old man. "Perhaps we shall have a campaign against that dog-brother Lucifer, and Saint Michael and Saint Wenceslaus will lead us under the Lord Jesus; and our Lady of Yasna Gora will look on when we come back victorious!"

And so they talked on until it was time to set the old man down, and Stanislaus mounted again to catch up with his party, which had gone ahead.

"With God!" cried the old man.

"With God!" echoed Stanislaus. 'And if you go to heaven before me, father, do not forget to plead for me with the Lord Jesus and with His Mother."

Then he clattered along the road, and shortly came up with Bilinski and Paul.

Sometimes they came to districts infested by robbers, and waited to join themselves to some larger party for protection. Sometimes they made long stretches of many hours in the saddle, when the inns were far apart and they could get no food on the road. Sometimes they tarried a day or two in a little town to rest their horses.

But everywhere Stanislaus thought of God, and prayed, and when occasion offered spoke of holy things as only he could speak. Bilinski and Paul often laughed at him, for they were of a different stamp. But he did not mind their ridicule, and he bore them no grudge for it. And so, after. many days, they came at length to Vienna, on July 26, 1564.

CHAPTER V
SCHOOL DAYS

Vienna WAS a great city, even in those days, since for a long time it had been the residence of the Roman Emperors of the West. It was a Catholic city, though even in 1564, little more than forty years after Luther's revolt, the Lutherans in the city had begun to be quite numerous.

The Society of Jesus had been founded in 1540, only ten years before Stanislaus was born. But it had spread quickly. For some years now there had been a Jesuit house in Vienna. In i560, four years before Stanislaus came to Vienna, the Emperor Ferdinand I had loaned to the Viennese Jesuits a large house next to their own, which they might use as a college. The Fathers built a connection between the two houses, so that they became practically one. Here they received boys from the city, from the country round about, even from Hungary and far Poland. Here Stanislaus took up his residence.

It was a simpler, less formal sort of school than we perhaps are accustomed to. The Fathers and the boys lived together, almost as one big family. They ate together in one large dining hall. There were always some of the Fathers with the boys in their games, as well as in their studies. It was a very pleasant place, and a very good place.

In those early days of Protestantism, Catholics, even Catholic boys, felt that they were in a fighting situation. The attacks upon the old faith woke new courage and devotion in those who remained faithful to the Church of the ages. And so, filled with that spirit of loyalty, that new earnestness which the times called forth, and living under the example of the simple manly piety of their Jesuit teachers, it is no wonder that the boys in the College of Vienna were an unusually good set of boys.

They had their regular classes, in languages, mathematics, and such science as the age knew. Latin was then the language of all educated people in Europe, the language of courts, the common meeting ground of all nations. Many a time, both in those days and later; a noble proved his rank and saved himself from mischance by the mere fact that he spoke Latin. It was not a dead language then, as it is now. It was in current use. Greek was comparatively new in Western schools. And though from their beginnings the Jesuits were famous teachers, we can hardly suppose that in their new and small college at Vienna the boys were much troubled by the speech of Plato and Demosthenes.

Of their games it is hard to know much at this late day. Sword-play and bouts of a soldierly sort were common enough. These boys were almost all of noble birth; most of them perhaps looked for-ward to the army for their profession. So they held mimic tournaments and played games in which they hurled lances through suspended rings; they shot with bows and arrows; and of course they had matches in running, jumping and wrestling.

We know that Stanislaus did uncommonly well in the schools. He was quick, had a good memory, and was too sensible to be lazy. And though the writers of his life say nothing about it, we are quite sure that he excelled in games and sports also. For one thing, he as a general favorite, esteemed by all his fellows; and that must mean that he was one with them in their play. For another, he was naturally no dreamer or moper, but the jolliest, cheeriest sort of boy. And finally, the boy who walked twelve hundred miles in a few weeks must have been well accustomed to using his legs. Try thirty miles a day on foot, day after day, you football players and baseball players, you trained athletes, and say whether it is the work of a weakling or of a boy who never played.

But it takes more than success in studies and in games to account for his great popularity with the other college boys. Such success may win a certain admiration and respect, but it does not of itself win friends. And Stanislaus had pretty nearly every one for his friend. To do that requires other gifts, gifts of character. Everybody liked him, because he had such gifts. He was pious, but not merely pious; much more than pious, he was good. That means he was unselfish. There is only one way to make people really love you, and that is to love them. That is what Stanislaus did; he loved the people he lived with. He was naturally good hearted, and big hearted. He had kept away from petty meannesses. He had fought down his natural selfishness. He had learned not to be always seeking his own little advantage, not to put himself forward for praise, not to insist on his " rights," not to boast and carry a high hand with his comrades, not to talk a lot about himself. He had learned to forgive little offenses, and big ones, too, for that matter. He knew all about how our Lord had suffered and put up with things and forgiven those who hurt Him. And he loved our Lord so much, was so much at home with Him, that almost without effort he acted as our Lord would want him to act. He had plenty of spirit, and a whole world of pluck and daring; but he was not quarrelsome. Then he was as cheerful as sunshine, and he made every one else cheerful. Why, the boys could not help loving a boy like him.

Sodalities were rare in those days; but the college boys of Vienna had a sodality, devoted to the honor of our Lady, and under the patronage of Saint Barbara. At their meetings; the sodalists in turn had to address their companions, give a little talk about the Blessed Virgin, or on some virtue, or the like.

Whenever Stanislaus' turn came, the boys were all expectation. He was no older than most of them; indeed, younger perhaps. But he had an older head. He had done more thinking than they, and a deal more praying. He had no false shame or babyish timidity. If he had anything to say, he was not afraid to say it. And he certainly had something to say. It had come to be as easy for him to talk about our Lady and heaven as for other boys to talk about their mothers at home. He had treasured up stories of the Blessed Virgin's help, with which Catholic Poland was filled. He spoke simply, unaffectedly, of our Lady's love for us, of her power, her willingness to aid us. And from him, though simply their school mate, the boys heard these things eagerly. He seemed well privileged to speak, as indeed he was.

To talk about pious things, and do it acceptably, is a mighty hard matter. You have to know how. And the first part of knowing how is to be at home with pious things, to have thought about them, often and long, to have woven them into your life as Stanislaus had done.

The trouble with us is that we live so far removed from thoughts of God, of His Mother, that they never cease to be strange to us. We go blunderingly about mention of them, or we lack the courage to speak at all. But why should they be strange or remote? We are destined to live forever in heaven, we are the daily recipients of

God's favors, we are sheltered, protected, every way by our Lady's loving care.

The things that touch us most nearly are the things of the spiritual world; they are the most thrillingly important; they are the only really important things. We are not afraid to talk baseball, or politics, or business. Why be afraid to talk of God's power, His dominion over us, His love for us, our duties to Him, the helps He gives us, the reward He holds out to us? There is only one answer: we don't think enough about these things. There is only one remedy: do thing about them, as Saint Stanislaus did.

CHAPTER VI
IN THE HOUSE OF KIMBERKER

The house which the Jesuits in Vienna used for their boarding college was not theirs. It belonged to the Emperor Ferdinand I, who had merely loaned it to them. Now the Emperor Ferdinand had died on July 25, 1564, the day before Paul and Stanislaus came to Vienna. The new Emperor, Maximilian II, left the house with the Jesuits for a time; but in March, 1565, withdrew it from their use. Of course, that meant the breaking up of the boarding-school. The Fathers still had their own residence, and they could teach a small number of day scholars. Many of their pupils went to their homes when they could no longer live with the Jesuits. Those who remained had to take lodgings elsewhere in the city.

It was decided that Paul and Stanislaus should be amongst the latter number. At once Bilinski set out with the two to get a house. In the Platz Kiemark, a fashionable quarter of the town, there was a splendid mansion, belonging to a Lutheran noble, the Senator Kimberker.

It took Paul's fancy immensely. On inquiry, they found that Kimberker used less than half of the house, for it was a huge building with many rooms, and that he was more than willing to rent the unused rooms to the young Poles. Stanislaus felt a little ill at ease over living with a Lutheran. But Bilinski and Paul pooh- poohed at his fears, and had their own way in the matter.

So in a few days they moved in, and fitted up a couple of the vacant rooms. Stanislaus was to live more than two years in this house, two years filled with a great deal of annoyance and pain, and yet blessed in wonderful ways. His difficulties began almost at once, and they were no slight difficulties. Of course, he and Paul went daily for classes to the Jesuits' house, and met daily the few boys who continued their studies in Vienna. But the old companionship, the old life of the boys in common, was gone. Only two or three of his best friends remained, and these were scattered through the city. He saw them for a little while after classes, he might now and then go out with them on a holiday. But for the most part he was thrown back upon the company of his tutor and his elder brother.

Both Paul and Bilinski liked a good time." They were far removed from the authority of home. Bilinski, who was in charge, was only a few years older than Paul; and whilst a good fellow in the main, was little able, or perhaps little willing, to put much check upon him.

And Paul was a pretty gay blade. Rough, boisterous, wild in manner, he picked companions like himself. Kimberker' 5 house soon became a noisy place. There were dinners at which the wine went round very freely, plenty of cards and dice, now and then brawling quarrels. It did not suit Stanislaus at all. He was too much of a gentleman, and too good, to act unpleasantly or resent the rough company that Paul brought home. But he could not mix freely with them, he did not like their talk or their manners, and he slipped quietly away from their noisy gatherings as soon as he decently could.

And so he was left alone; and lonesomeness for a boy of fourteen is a very unpleasant thing. He still did well in his classes, but he was no book-worm. When he had done his duty in study, the books had no further claim upon him, and no attraction in themselves. And yet he kept up his wonderful brightness and cheeriness all the time; so that Bilinski often wondered at him. And it was worth wondering at, for there is nothing, as everybody knows, which sooner breaks down one's spirits and brings on the blue devils than being left alone, without friends and companionship.

How did he do it? The fact is, he refused to be alone. As his friends in Vienna left him, he simply turned more to his friends in heaven. And heaven came down to him. Any old vacant room in the big, half-empty house was his chapel. And through the long, lonely days, often through great part of the night, he prayed.

If you could have seen him pray! Imagine any good-hearted boy who has been away from home for a long stretch, say a couple of years, and who comes back and meets father, mother, brothers, sisters. He may not say much, but he LOOKS a good deal, and he feels more than any words can say. That is the way Stanislaus prayed. He just turned to God and his Mother in heaven, with all his love in his eyes and immense happiness in his heart. And if he spoke, or said things to them in his mind, he could speak simply, like a little child, because no one else would hear him and he would not need be shy or bashful.

If you could have seen him pray, you would never think, as so many do, that praying is a gloomy business. His face was lit up, his eyes bright, his whole body spoke of peace and courage and joy. He kept thinking so much about heaven that he seemed to live there in advance. Everybody knows how, when the school year is nearly over and vacations are at hand, there is a joyful atmosphere about the days. Lessons do not seem so hard, though they really are just the same old lessons. Classes seem to have more life and spirit in them. Boys are in better temper. Every detail of work and play is colored by expectation, as if the relief of vacation were already foretasted. Stanislaus looked forward just that way to the Great Vacation, to going Home forever. He knew that even the longest life. ends soon, that all its difficulties and troubles pass away and eternity begins; and he felt so light-hearted looking ahead to that eternity that nothing happening here could sadden him - except sin, and he kept away from that.

Paul and his boisterous fellows thought that Paul's younger brother was a queer chap. But they liked him, just the same, because he was always pleasant and smiling. He never said a word to them about their conduct. But when they talked to him, he naturally spoke of the things he was always thinking about. And they did not like that. Such talk tended to stir up their consciences, even to frighten them. And they did not want their con-sciences stirred up. You can often see that. You may have noticed in yourself that, if you are not living as you ought to live, any word about God or death or heaven or our Blessed Lady irritates you, makes you feel horribly uncomfortable. And so Stanislaus became a puzzle to them, because they would not see. And little by little they left him alone, or only spoke to him to tease him or make fun of him.

CHAPTER VII
THE TEST OF COURAGE

Paul was the worst at this teasing; nor did it stop at mere teasing. He was not a really bad fellow, but he was selfish, set upon having his own will in everything, and had a very quick and fierce temper. Stanislaus' quiet refusal to join in the noisy revels of himself and his companions, his unaffected piety, his long hours of prayer, were things he could not understand. They seemed a sort of standing rebuke to him, and they constantly nettled him. Of course he sought reasons to justify himself, as we all do when we are in the wrong. When they were alone, he and Bilinski fell to scolding Stanislaus.

"You shame us!" Paul would cry. "You do not act like a nobleman, but like some boorish peasant."

Then Stanislaus would be troubled. He knew he was in the right. He simply could not stand the free ways and freer speech of Paul and his companions. But how could he justify himself? How could he defend his own position without at least seeming to attack his brother's? And that last he would never do. S6metimes he tried to smooth matters over by saying:

"We take different ways, Paul. I do not condemn yours. Why not let me alone in mine?"

But oftenest he could only smile and say nothing. And whether he answered or kept silence, Paul was sure to grow more irritated. Then Bilinski tried to exert his authority.

"Your father gave you into my charge," he would say. "I order you to act like the rest of us and not make yourself odd and shame us by your conduct."

But Stanislaus knew well enough what were the limits of Bilinski's authority and he was not at all the sort of boy to be easily bullied by a mere assumption of authority that did not exist.

The result always was that Stanislaus continued to do what his own conscience urged him to do, and that Bilinski and Paul felt helpless in the face of his quiet, fearless persistence. And that made them the more vexed with him. They nicknamed him "The Jesuit," they mimicked him, they sneered at him. He had a pretty hot temper himself, but he kept himself well in hand, and was always kind and pleasant with these cross-grained comrades. He was not the least bit afraid. Whenever he thought that speaking would do any good, he spoke up without hesitation. Many a time, when Paul taunted him with acting in a way to bring discredit upon his name, he answered:

"No man shames his name by trying to please God. As for what men may think or say, that does not matter much. Do you think we shall bother much about that in eternity?"

There were two cousins of theirs who often stayed with the Kostkas; one of them was also called Stanislaus, the other, who afterwards rose to high rank in his native country, was named Rozrarewski. These sided with Paul and did their best to help him in making Stanislaus' life miserable.

It was not long before Paul went on from words to blows. One day Stanislaus quietly tried to answer some of Paul's sneers. Paul sprang at him in a rage and, striking out savagely, knocked him down. Bilinski interfered, and when he had drawn off Paul, proceeded to scold Stanislaus as being the cause of all the trouble. Such meanness and injustice must have made the boy's blood boil. But he mastered himself and said nothing.

That afternoon Paul was going out riding. He could not find his spurs. "Take mine," said Stanislaus, pleasantly, as if nothing had happened. And Paul took them, a little ashamed, saying to himself:

"He's a decent little beggar, after all - if only he weren't so insufferably pious!"

But Paul, though he might be touched for the moment by his brother's readiness to forgive, continued to grow even more irritated with him. Many and many a time he struck Stanislaus; and often, after knocking him down, kicked him and then tramped on him. And Bilinski always took the same line, trying to make peace by blaming everything on Stanislaus.

Now Stanislaus was very nearly Paul's equal in size, and easily his match in strength. He lived simply and frugally, kept himself in condition, did not over-eat and over-drink as Paul did. He could, without much difficulty, have met Paul's brutality in kind, and very likely have given him a good beating. And he knew well enough that if he did so, Paul would let him alone. For when was there ever a bully who was not also a coward?

And you may be sure he felt like doing it. He was in the right, and knew he was. He was high-spirited and utterly without fear. And yet he never even defended himself. lie let Paul bully him and beat him. He endured to have himself looked upon as a coward - although you may observe that all the time he did not budge an inch from the line of conduct he had chosen. And why? Well, for a lot of reasons.

In the first place, he kept saying to himself, "What difference does it make for eternity? Then, he knew his own high temper and he would not let himself go, for fear he should commit a sin - and he hated sin with all his soul.

And then he recalled what our Lord had suffered for him, and he said:

"If you will give me the courage to stand it, I'll be glad, Lord, to suffer this much for You."

And that last was the reason why, in the midst of this real persecution, he never lost his cheerfulness. More than that, he never missed a chance to do Paul and his friends a good turn. He said:

"When men were treating our Lord worst, even killing Him, that was when He was opening heaven for them. And I'm sure He would like me to be kind as He was kind to those who treated Him meanly."

He did what he could to avoid annoying Paul. He kept out of everybody's way when he wanted to pray. He used to wait at night till the others were asleep, for they all slept in one great room together, and then slip out of bed and on to his knees. Sometimes his cousins, thinking it a great joke, would pretend to stumble over him in the half-dark, and kick him as hard as they could.

And this went on for two years. He could have stopped the whole matter with no trouble at all, by simply writing to his father. But he never so much as hinted to any one at home of the way Paul and Bilinski and his cousins treated him. He was as plucky as he was gentle and forgiving. Although, for good reasons, he would not quarrel, he had the tenacity of a bull-dog, he held on to the hard purpose he had formed and nothing could beat him off.

And that is the very highest sort of courage, the courage that endures, that has no show or heroics about it. Again I say, if he had done all this, put up with all this, to gain riches, to make a name for himself, the world would understand and would praise him tremendously. It is his motive that leaves the world cold, it is the source and reason of his courage that the world cannot understand.

Yet he was not obstinate and pig-headed, bound to do as he wished just because he wished it. No, he was very sensible and did everything with reason. He would not stop saying his prayers when Bilinski and Paul objected, he would not join in gay dinners and drinking-bouts and gambling, he would not sit and smile at shady stories or smutty wit. He would no? do anything his conscience forbade. But he was most ready to do anything else they wanted.

For instance, he had been used to give his rich clothes away to the poor, and dress very simply. Bilinski and Paul insisted on his dressing as became his rank, and he yielded readily. Bilinski wanted him to take dancing lessons, and he took them, and learned to dance very well. He was not keen about any of these things, because he reckoned they would not count for much in eternity. But neither was he foolish, nor a fanatic, nor one who saw evil where no evil was. He was simply a level-headed boy, who figured out the business of life clearly and convincingly, and who had the courage of a hero in living up to his convictions.

CHAPTER VIII
IN DANGER OF DEATH

Two years of loneliness; when his brother and his cousins and his tutor, who should have been his comrades, were his persecutors; two years in which he was always under a strain, always having to control his anger, to be patient and sweet-tempered amidst a thousand vexations; two years, moreover, in which the bodily exercise he was used to, and which he needed as every growing boy needs it, was cut down to a minimum; two such years would have broken the health even of a grown, strong man. And Stanislaus was not a grown, strong man, but a boy of sixteen. It is remarkable that he should have held out so long. It shows what courage and goodness and trust in God can do. But finally, towards the end of November, 1566, his body and brain could stand it no longer. He fell sick, with fever.

He was not a baby. He did not complain, or even tell any one that he felt unwell. He kept to his feet for weeks, trying to go on as usual with his work and his prayers. The feast of Saint Barbara, who had been the patroness of the boys' sodality in Vienna, was drawing near. Stanislaus prepared for it with particular care and devotion. Saint Barbara was the patroness of a happy death and her clients always besought of her the special grace of receiving the Holy Viaticum when dying.

December 4th, the feast of the Saint, came and passed. Stanislaus grew weaker, his fever increased. About the middle of the month he had to keep his bed, and his condition quickly became serious. Then Bilinski and Paul forgot their anger against the boy. They called in the best physicians of the city, they spared no pains or expense. The servants, who had always loved this gentle master, were all kindness and attention. But despite the efforts of all, Stanislaus became steadily worse.

He was entirely at peace, not at all afraid. Yet he felt that death was coming near. He prayed whole hours, smiling gladly in talk with our Lord, with the Blessed Virgin, with his guardian angel. He was ready, even eager, to go home. The evil spirit wondered at this boy of sixteen, who had fought him off so bravely through his life and who was dying now so fearlessly.

One day, when his people and even the servants had left him for a little while, Stanislaus saw an enormous black dog with glaring eyes and hideous foaming jaws rush across the room toward his bed. The door was closed. It was impossible for the beast to have entered the room in any ordinary way. Stanislaus had no notion how it could have come there. But if he was frightened for the moment, he did not lose his wits. With an effort, he sat up in bed and made the sign of the cross. "In the name of the Father, Son and Holy Ghost!" he cried aloud. Instantly the huge, snarling dog fell to the floor with a thud as if struck by a sword. But after a few moments he sprang up again, and first circling the room, came crouching to the bed, howling as no mortal dog could howl, making ready to spring at the sick boy. Again Stanislaus made the sign of the cross. Again the terrible dog was stricken to the floor. A third time he came, only to be beaten back in the same way. And then, standing with bristling hair and horrible cries in the middle of the room, he vanished from sight. Stanislaus fell back on the bed, fearfully exhausted, and with tears in his eyes thanked God for his deliverance.

The shock of this dreadful incident prostrated him. He failed more and more. The doctors, coming several times a day, shook their heads in despair.

"We can do no more," they said, "the end is now only a question of time."

For seven days and nights Bilinski sat by his bed, snatching only a few hours' sleep now and then, for he feared that Stanislaus might die any moment.

Yet in all this long time they had brought no priest to the dying boy. Every day he begged them earnestly that he might receive the Holy Viaticum. But they lied to him. Bilinski said:

"You will soon be well. The doctors will cure you. Don't think of death or go frightening yourself."

"I am not afraid," said Stanislaus. "But I know I am dying. Do not let me die without Holy Communion."

But Bilinski still put him off, and tried to tease him jokingly with charges of cowardice.

The fact was, Bilinski and Paul were afraid of their Lutheran landlord, the Senator Kimberker. His anti-Catholic prejudice was intense. They feared he might put them, sick boy and all, out of his house, if they dared to bring a priest and the Blessed Sacrament into it.

That was a hard trial for Stanislaus. But he met it as he had met every difficulty, bravely, hopefully, cheerfully. He remembered Saint Barbara, of whom he had asked 'the grace of not dying without the Holy Viaticum. He renewed his prayers for her intercession. He laid his whole case with confidence before God, and with confidence waited.

Bilinski still sat by his bed, watching anxiously. The day passed, the light failed, darkness and night came on. Stanislaus all the time had lain quiet, his face smiling as ever, his lips moving in prayer. Suddenly he turned to Bilinski, radiant, glowing with joy.

"Kneel down, kneel down!" he said, in a clear but low voice. "Two angels of God are bringing the Blessed Sacrament, and with them comes Saint Barbara!"

Then, worn out though he was by his long sickness, Stanislaus raised himself, knelt on the bed, and struck his breast as he three times repeated:

"Lord, I am not worthy!"

Then he raised his face, and opening his lips received his sacramental Lord. Bilinski looked on with awe and almost terror, unable to say a word. Stanislaus, when he had received the Blessed Sacrament, lay down again in bed and began his thanksgiving.

He was more than ever ready for death now. But still death held off. All the next day he passed in quiet. The doctors said:

"Now is the end. He may die at any moment."

But he was not to die yet. Toward evening our Lady herself came to him, carrying in her arms the Infant Jesus. The sick boy looked up in wonder and delight. There was his Mother, smiling at him, and in her arms the laughing Infant. The divine Child stretched out His little hands to Stanislaus, and Stanislaus, sitting up in his bed, took Him into his arms.

What passed in his soul then, what joy filled his heart, we cannot know until we shall come to heaven and taste for ourselves of that joy.

And the Blessed Virgin and the Child Jesus spoke to him and comforted him.

But Stanislaus was too overcome to say anything. Only tears streamed down from his eyes as he pressed the Infant Savior to his breast.

Our Lady said to him:

"You must end your days in the Society that bears my Son's name. You must be a Jesuit."

But so soon as he had taken the Infant into his arms, Stanislaus felt that the fever left him, his strength came back, the blood coursed through his body with a new sense of vigor and vitality.

Then our Lady received her Child back from his hands, smiled at him and blessed him, and so vanished from his sight.

Stanislaus called for his clothes, dressed and got up. Bilinski and Paul and the doctors were astounded.

"It cannot be!" they cried.

"But you see that it is," said Stanislaus. "I am as well as ever. Our Lady and the little Jesus came and cured me. And now I must go to the church and thank them."

Nor did the fever return. He was entirely recovered.

The house in which this occurred is now a sanctuary, and in the room in which Stanislaus had received such favors from God an altar stands, and above it a statue of the Saint.

CHAPTER IX
VOCATION

When our Lady came to cure Stanislaus, she told him absolutely that he must become a Jesuit. That was not the first idea Stanislaus had had of his vocation. Even some months before his illness he had felt himself drawn to enter the Society of Jesus. But now, all doubts removed, he made a vow in thanksgiving to obey our Lady's command.

He went to his confessor, the Jesuit Father Doni, and told him of the vision of the Blessed Virgin and her order to become a Jesuit. Father Doni believed him readily enough, but he said:

"I can do nothing myself in the matter. You must go to the Provincial, for only he can admit you. But I am afraid there will be difficulties."

Stanislaus was not merely afraid, he was quite certain, there would be difficulties. However, he assured Father Doni:

"Even if there be no end of difficulties, still I shall be a Jesuit. Since our Lady has commanded me, she will find a way."

The Provincial, Father Laurence Maggi, received Stanislaus kindly, of course, yet with anything but encouragement. There had been trouble for the Society shortly before, though in another place, because of some novices admitted without their parents' consent. The Provincial did not wish to risk having a like disturbance brought about his own ears.

"But the Blessed Virgin will take care of the whole business, Father," said Stanislaus. "She will quiet any opposition my father may make."

Well, the Provincial was willing to believe that too. But he knew that God wants us to use our own common sense and not to act rashly and then rely upon Him, or upon our Lady's intercession with Him, to get us out of scrapes. So he had to give the only answer which prudence could give, to all Stanislaus' petitions.

"You must either get your father's permission, or you must wait until you are of age and your own master." Now, Stanislaus was quite certain his father would not hear for a moment of his becoming a Jesuit. On the other hand, he did not want to wait four or five years until he should come of age. He had that peculiar courage, which many people cannot understand at all, the courage to be afraid. He was very much afraid, afraid to trifle with God's grace, afraid lest if he did not take the favor now when it was offered him, it might not be offered another time.

He thought of another means of persuading the Provincial. The Apostolic Legate of Pope Saint Pius V to the court of the Emperor at Vienna was Cardinal Commendoni. This Cardinal had been Nuncio, and afterwards Legate, to Poland, and had come from Poland only a year or so before. He was well acquainted with the Lord John Kostka and with Stanislaus. When he came to Vienna, Paul and Stanislaus had visited him, and Stanislaus had made the Cardinal, as he did most people, his friend. So he went to Cardinal Commendoni. He figured hopefully that, as the Cardinal was the Pope's representative, he could easily impose his will on the Jesuit Provincial; and of course he would do so as his friend.

Commendoni welcomed the boy, listened to him attentively, marvelled at his unaffected goodness and at the heavenly favors shown him. Stanislaus told him of the distressing obstinacy of the Provincial.

"But how about your father?" the Cardinal asked.

"Oh, my father is more hopeless than the Provincial," Stanislaus answered. "If I so much as mentioned the matter to him, he would bring me back to Poland, and I should have no chance at all."

As Commendoni knew the Lord John pretty well, he said nothing to that. But he thought to himself that Stanislaus was fairly accurate in his forecast.

After a moment's thought, he said:

"You certainly have a right to follow your vocation. God's will comes before even your father's. But it is not going to be easy. However, I shall speak to the Father Provincial, and do what I can."

Stanislaus went away with good hopes. He was to return in a few days to hear the result of Commendoni's plea. But when he came back to the Cardinal, he found only another disappointment. The Provincial not merely was as stubborn as ever, he had even won the Cardinal to his way of thinking. It was too risky to admit him, it was altogether unwise.

Most boys might have given up after that. Stanislaus did not give up. He was quite sure of what God wanted, and difficulties simply did not count. lie was called to be a Jesuit, and a Jesuit he would be. If he could not gain admission into the Society in Vienna, well, he would try elsewhere.

But even with his mind fairly made up, he sought more guidance. A young Portuguese Jesuit, Father Antoni, had lately come to Vienna as preacher to the Empress Maria. Every one was talking about his ability, his prudence, his zeal. Stanislaus went to him, and laid his troubles before him.

Father Antoni took some little time to think it all over, then decided very definitely. He called Stanislaus to him.

"Do you understand," he asked, "what it will mean to go away, to leave your people, to live in a strange country?"

Stanislaus said, yes, he understood perfectly.

"And that you are closing the door on your return, that in no case will you ever be received again at Kostkov?"

Yes, Stanislaus knew that too.

"And that you will have to go an immense journey on foot, with plenty of hardships; to find at the end of it a life that is not easy, to live at the beck and call of another, to do menial work, to endure humiliations, to sacrifice everything that the world holds. dear?"

Stanislaus smiled at him. He had reckoned it all out, he had "counted the cost" long before, he was ready.

Then, in God's name, go! " said Father Antonie "And may God be with you in all. I'll give you letters to Father Canisius, the Provincial in Augsburg, and to Father Francis Borgia, the General, who is in Rome."

Then Stanislaus was happy. At last he was in a fair way to obey the command of God, which our Lady herself had brought him. Father Antoni spoke with him longer, pointed out in detail many of the difficulties that awaited him, gave him counsel for the road. Then he went to write the letters of introduction, and Stanislaus went back to Paul and Bilinski and their blows and sneers, to get ready for his tramp.

CHAPTER X
THE RUNAWAY

He was going to run away. But he was not going to sneak away. He was just as kind and forgiving to Paul as he had always been. He bore him no ill-will for his three years of abuse, now that he had determined upon a course of action, which would free him from a continuance of it. He had often felt angry over Paul's treatment of him, but he had kept down his anger under his vigorous will.

But now he made up his mind that Paul would receive something of a shock the next time he had resort to his now almost habitual amusement of beating his younger brother. Meantime, he bought a peasant's tunic and a pair of rough shoes that would be serviceable for his long march.

It was not long before something or other Stanislaus did or said woke Paul's easily aroused rage. He began with oaths, of which he seemed to possess a pretty stock. He worked himself up into greater and greater heat of temper - a substitute for courage with many people. Finally he sprang at Stanislaus. Formerly, on such occasions Stanislaus was so busy holding his own temper in check that he could do little else, he stood almost like a statue. But this time Paul felt there was something wrong. Stanislaus was looking straight at him. When he leaped to strike him, Stanislaus quietly and skillfully thrust him aside. Paul stumbled, staggered, recovered himself. But when he looked again, fear took hold of him. He was afraid of what he saw in Stanislaus' eyes. The younger boy spoke quietly, coolly.

"That will be about enough," he said; "I've put up with your cowardice and brutality for three years. I'll stand it no longer. Since I cannot have peace here, well,. I'll look for it somewhere else. You can answer to our father, and tell him how it happened."

Paul was still frightened. The situation was extremely novel to him. The turning of the worm! What would happen next! He was afraid at first that Stanislaus was going to give him his long-due payment, and he had no stomach to face the reckoning. He had not noticed before how wiry and strong Stanislaus looked. But when he saw that the boy made no movement, only spoke in that quiet voice, he plucked up a little courage. He began to bluster and swear.

"You'll go away, will you?" he cried. "What the devil do I care? Go, and be hanged to you!" - that was the gist of it, only a trifle more ornamental.

"Don't forget! " said Stanislaus. " Send word to father. I'm certainly going away."

Paul was waxing eloquent again, but Stanislaus turned on his heel and walked away. Nor did the bullying big brother venture to follow him. He contented himself with calling him hard names which he could not hear, and muttering savagely to himself for some time. But, naturally, he did not believe at all that Stanislaus was really going to run away9 He looked upon the words as an empty threat.

And so it was all over. Stanislaus sighed a sigh of relief. There was nothing ahead of him now save the road to Augsburg. He said his prayers tranquilly and went to bed.

Morning came, or the dawn that precedes the morning. Stanislaus got up, selected his finest suit of clothes, and dressed. His first care was to write the letter for Paul and his father. This he put between the leaves of a book.

The servants, of course, even in the primitive housekeeping of the Kostkas, slept in another room than the big common apartment of their masters. Stanislaus went to the bed of one of them, named Pacifici, who was rather particularly devoted to him, and who afterwards became a Franciscan. He shook Pacifici and woke him. The servant rubbed his eyes sleepily, then gazed in astonishment at the brilliant figure standing in the half-light beside his bed. What was the Lord Stanislaus doing, dressed in this unusual finery, at such an unearthly hour!

"Listen," said Stanislaus, "I am going out for the day. I have received an invitation which I must accept. I am going now. If Bilinski or the Lord Paul ask for me, tell them that."

"I will, your grace, I will," said Pacifici. But he was almost too astonished to speak.

Stanislaus left the room and the house. He walked quickly to the Jesuit church, where he heard Mass and received Holy Communion. At Mass he met a young Hungarian, with whom he had been very intimate. He beckoned him aside and whispered:

"Wait for me a minute. I just want to say a word to Father Antoni."

Then he hurried away, but was back shortly at his friend's side, eyes dancing, lips smiling, hand outstretched.

"I have just bid Father Antoni good-by," he said, with a little excitement. "I am running away. I am going to Augsburg' to ask admission into the Society of Jesus. I told Paul yesterday that I should not stay with him, and I have written a letter and put it in a book. Do not tell any one what I tell you now. But after a few days, please go and point out the letter to Paul."

His friend listened with wonder. Going away!' Going to Augsburg!

"But how?" he asked. "Not on foot?"

"On foot, to be sure," answered Stanislaus gayly. "Do you think I have a horse secreted about me? Or could I take one of ours and wake the house?"

"And you will be a Jesuit, and teach, and never ride a good horse again, and give up your people and your place in the world!"

"I shall be a Jesuit, if I can," said Stanislaus. "As for what I shall give up, well, I'd have to give it up when death came, wouldn't I? And since God wants it, I'd sooner give it up now."

But he had not much time for talk. Day was growing; he must be off. He got his friend's promise about the letter, bade him good-by heartily and cheerily, and turned his face towards the Augsburg road. What happened else that day we have already seen, and how Paul and Bilinski followed him, and how he got away, and how he did walk, bravely, gayly, in less than two weeks the four hundred miles to Augsburg.

CHAPTER XI
AT DILLIGEN

It was well on in the afternoon of August 30th or 31st when Stanislaus arrived at Augsburg. The town was strange to him. He had to ask his way to the Jesuit house.

"I want to see Father Canisius," he told the porter at the door. "I have a letter of introduction to him."

The porter was very sorry, but Father Canisius was not in Augsburg. Stanislaus' heart fell. Not in Augsburg! His four hundred miles on foot for nothing! It was a terrible disappointment.

"Wait a moment," said the porter, "until I call one of the Fathers."

As Stanislaus waited, he kept asking himself, "What shall I do? What shall I do now?" And for a little while he could not think clearly. He felt almost sick. But he was not the kind to be discouraged long, and before the porter returned with the Father he had made up his mind.

"Since Canisius is not in Augsburg, well, I'll go to whatever place he is in.

The Father who came was all regrets. Canisius had gone to Dillingen. But would not Stanislaus come in, and at least rest a few days before seeking him further? No, Stanislaus was going on - at once.

"How far is it?" he asked. "And can you point me out the road?"

"It is about thirty-five miles," the Father answered. "But you can't go on this evening. You must be dreadfully tired."

Yes, he was tired, but not so tired that he could not go to Dillingen.

It is only a little way, after all," he said, smiling as he always smiled. But he stopped to eat something with the Jesuits, both because he was hungry, and because it would be discourteous to refuse all their kind offers.

One of the lay-brothers had to go on business to Dillingen, so he hastened to accompany Stanislaus. It is from his testimony that we know what happened on the way.

Before the sun had quite set, he was on the road once more. He slept in a field that night. He was up early the next morning, and stepped out bravely, fasting, and hoping for a chance to go to Holy Communion.

The evening before, he had left Augsburg a good many miles behind. A few miles more in the early morning brought him to a little village. From some distance he saw the spire of its church. He hastened his steps, lest Mass should be over before he reached the place.

When he came to the church, he saw through its open door a scattered little congregation at their prayers. He entered quickly, sank to his knees, and dropping his face between his hands began to pray. But somehow the place felt strange. After a bit he looked about him, and saw with astonishment that he was in a Lutheran church. The Lutheran heresy was still young and kept up many Catholic practices. It was easy to be deceived.

He felt a little shocked. He had been preparing to receive Holy Communion, and now he should have to go without. But as he looked about, the church to his eyes glowed with light. Out of the light came a troop of blessed angels and drew near to him. He was frightened, delighted, all at once. Then he saw that one of the angels bore with deep reverence the Blessed Sacrament, and that God had granted his desire for Holy Communion. He received It with quiet joy, but simply, humbly, for he knew that this miracle of Its coming to him was as nothing to the miracle that there should be any Blessed Sacrament at all. Since God had stooped to leave us His Flesh and Blood, the manner in which He gave It was of quite secondary importance.

It would have astounded us to be in his place in the little Lutheran church that morning. We try to fancy how we should feel, if we too saw a host of angels approach us. Yet every day we may avail ourselves of that more wonderful miracle, before which even visions of angels pale - the miracle of having God Himself for our Meat and Drink.

That day brought him to Dillingen and Peter Canisius, the "Watch-dog of Germany," as he was called, for his vigilance against heresy. Canisius read the letter of

Father Antoni, and listened to Stanislaus' story. It was all quite wonderful. As the boy talked, Canisius looked at him and studied him: not quite seventeen, lively, handsome, full of spirit and daring, quick in speech, eager, affectionate, pious.

You might call Canisius a man of war, an old veteran. His hair had grown gray in battles of the soul, in fighting back heresy, in strengthening weak hearts through that age of trial. He knew the value of enthusiasm, but he knew its weakness, too.

"A very taking lad," he thought to himself. "He flashes like a rapier. But will his metal stand hard use?"

It was the thought of common sense. He did not mistrust Stanislaus. But, on the other hand, what did he know about him? He had not much to go by as yet; only Antoni's letter, and the boy's engaging presence. He would take no definite step about admitting Stanislaus into the Society until he did know more.

"Yon want to be a Jesuit?" he said, with thoughtful brows. "When?"

It was on Stanislaus' tongue to say, "Now, at once." But he hesitated a moment, and said instead, "As soon as you think fit."

You are a stranger to us, you know," Canisius went on, smiling a little, but pleasantly. "And before we admit men amongst us, we need to know that they have something more than a mere desire to join us.. That takes time to find out. Are you willing to stop in the college here for a while?"

Stanislaus answered promptly, "Of course I am."

"Not as a student," said Canisius. "But as a servant?"

"As anything you want," Stanislaus agreed.

"Well, come with me," Canisius said, and he led the way to the kitchen.

"Here's a new cook," he said to the brother in charge. "At least, he may have in him the makings of a cook. Can you give him something to do?"

It was not a very encouraging reception, although it was not so bad as it may sound, condensed as it is in these pages. Neither was it meant to be encouraging. It was meant to test.

Stanislaus was as cheerful as a lark. He rolled up his sleeves, smiled at the brother, and waited orders. The brother smiled back, and said:

"First, I think you will have something to eat. Then we shall see about work."

The Jesuit college at Dillingen, Saint Jerome's, was a big place and numbered many students. Many students mean many cooks and servers at table and servants about the house. Stanislaus took his place amongst a score of such. He washed dishes, helped prepare food, swept, scrubbed -whatever he was told to do. He ate with the servants, took his recreations with them. And he went about it all as simply and naturally as if he had been doing nothing else all his life.

His jolliness and kindness won him friends on all sides, as they had always done. He kept up his prayers, you may be sure; ran in to visit our Lord in the Blessed Sacrament whenever he was free to do so; made all he did into a prayer. And of course that irritated some of the other servants, just as it had irritated his brother Paul. And so he had no lack of teasing and petty insults. But he just smiled his way through them and kept on.

He was perfectly happy, entirely confident that he was doing God's will. As for the work, he chuckled to himself at the idea that Canisius thought this a test! He would willingly do a thousand times harder things than that for Almighty God. And after all, he said, it really was not so hard. Many a better man than he had to work much harder, at much more unpleasant tasks. And what would it matter in eternity, if he scrubbed pots and pans and floors and windows all his life? The only thing that mattered was to please God, and just now this sort of work was what pleased God.

CHAPTER XII
THE ROAD TO ROME

anisius kept Stanislaus at his work in the kitchen and about the house for a couple of weeks. He noted his cheerfulness, his love of prayer, his readiness to do any sort of work, and best of all, his simplicity, his entire lack of pose. He saw that this Senator's son made no virtue of taking on himself such lowly tasks, and he knew, therefore, that he was really humble.

Then he called the boy to him. He said:

"If I admit you into the Society here, your father may still annoy you. It is better you should go to Rome and become a novice there. I shall give you a letter to the Father General, Francis Borgia. In a few days two of ours are to go to Rome. You can go with them."

Stanislaus was delighted. He was come into quiet waters at last. But Canisius spoke further:

"First, however, you must get some decent clothes. Your old tunic," he said, with a twinkle in his eye, "might do well enough for a noble, but not for a future Jesuit."

So the college tailor made Stanislaus a simple, neat suit of clothes. And about September 20th he set out for Rome. He went on foot, of course; in the company of Jacopo Levanzio, a Genoese, and Fabricius Reiner, of Liége.

They struck south through Bavaria to the Tyrolese Alps. By what pass they crossed the Alps we do not know. But Stanislaus saw first from afar the white peaks, with their everlasting snows, shining in the sun. Then he went up and up, into cooler and rarer air, where one's lungs expand and one's step is light and buoyant, but where one gets tired more easily than in the plains. High up in the passes he felt the cold of Winter, although it was as yet early Autumn.

Then he came down the southern slopes of the great mountain-wall that locks in Italy, and with him came the headwaters of great rivers. He came down through bare rocks, then through twisted mountain-pines, then through green and lovely valleys, and so into the plains of northern Italy. He saw the mountain torrents leap and flash, and grow always bigger and stronger. He saw them slack their speed and widen their beds in the upland valleys. He saw them grow sluggish, tawny with mud, in the plain.

He saw the many spires of Milan's wonderful cathedral as they drew near the city. And when they tarried there a little while for rest, he saw the famous armor made there, hung up for show in little shop- windows. He passed great cavalcades of nobles and soldiers, and marvelled at their straight, slim rapiers, so different from the heavy Polish saber. He heard Italian speech for the first time, and tried to get at its meaning through his Latin.

But he and his companions had not over-much time for observing. They were traveling pretty swiftly. From Dillingen to Rome is a matter of about eight hundred miles. They left Dillingen September 20th; they reached Rome October 25th. That figures out to an average of about twenty-two miles each day. Then, if you remember that they had to climb mountains the first part of the way, that there were delays entering towns, delays of devotion when they came to great churches, you can see that many a day they must have equaled or surpassed Stanislaus' thirty miles a day from Vienna.

But it was pleasanter. for Stanislaus than his first great tramp. Now he had two good companions, with whom he could speak easily and familiarly of the things nearest his heart. He had none of the uncertainty about the result of this journey which he had had about his former journey. He found shelter and friendship in many Jesuit houses on the way.

As the three went on they lightened the road with pious songs, they heard Mass and received Holy Communion whenever occasion offered, they knelt by many a wayside shrine, a crucifix, or statue of our Lady, scattered everywhere through Catholic Italy.

It did not take the two Jesuits long to appreciate Stanislaus and delight in his company. He was so light-hearted, so merry in all the discomforts and hardships of the long road, so thoroughly and simply good. They wondered at his physical endurance, at the ease and buoyancy with which the lad of seventeen kept up that hard march, day after day.

The grasses of the Campagna were brown and brittle, the trees sere and yellow in the Autumn, when they came to the Eternal City, the center of the world then as now. The saintly General Francis Borgia, busy as he was with the cares of the widespread Society, found time to welcome the three travelers, and to hear Stanislaus' wonderful story in full.

And this time there was no hesitation or delay. Stanislaus entered his name in the book containing the register of the novices, on October 25, 1567. Three days later he received his cassock and entered at once upon his noviceship.

There were so many novices in Rome then that no single house of the Jesuits there could hold them all. So they were scattered through three houses, each one spending a part of his two years' noviceship successively in each house. Stanislaus went first to the Professed House, then called Santa Maria della Strada, and afterward the site of the famous Gesu, one of the notable churches of Rome. From there he passed in time to the Roman College, then to the Noviciate proper at Sant' Andrea.

The Society of Jesus was then in its early youth, in the midst of that first brilliant charge against the ranks of heresy without, and against the huge sluggish inertia so striking within the Church itself.

He was fellow-novice with Claude Acquaviva, son of the Duke of Atri, and afterwards one of the greatest Generals of the Society, which he ruled for thirty years. With him were also Claude's nephew, Rudolph Acquaviva, who died a martyr; Torres, a great theologian; Prando, the first philosopher at the University of Bologna; Fabio de' Fabii, who traced his descent from the great Roman family of that name; the Pole, Warscewiski, formerly ambassador to the Sultan and Secretary of State in Poland, who first wrote a life of Stanislaus; and many more, distinguished for birth, learning, holiness.

Most of these were a great deal older, too, than Stanislaus. Many of them had already made their names familiar to men. Yet the boy of seventeen, who came quietly and modestly amongst them, was somehow soon looked up to by all. They felt the force of something in him which made him their superior. Heaven was wonderfully near him. He was not old-fashioned; he was always a boy, unconscious of anything unusual in himself; not solemn nor impressive nor austere in manner. All that he did, he did with perfect naturalness; for to him the supernatural had become almost natural.

CHAPTER XIII
THE NOVICESHIP

Most of us, perhaps, think of the saints as men and women who accomplished visibly great things. Saint Paul, Saint Augustine, Saint Patrick, Saint Theresa, Saint Philip Neri, Saint Francis Xavier: such names as these come first to our minds when we think of "a saint." Yet the fact is that the greater number of saints are men and women who never did anything that the world would consider great or striking. Saint Joseph was of that sort. Even the Blessed Virgin lived and died in obscurity, made no stir in the world.

Sanctity is measured not so much by what one does as by how one does all things. Externally a saint may not differ at all from other people. It is his soul that is different.

And so, a visitor to the Professed House in Rome in 1567, meeting Stanislaus Kostka, would see a handsome, pleasant-looking Polish boy of seventeen, with his sleeves rolled up above his elbows, with an apron over his cassock, carrying wood for the kitchen fires, washing dishes, serving at table, sweeping corridors and rooms.

He got up at half past four, or five o'clock, every morning. He spent half an hour in meditation, in thinking over some incident in our Lord's life or some great truth, as that death is near to each of us, that this life is only the vestibule of eternity, that our whole business in life is to do what God wants us to do, or the like.

After that came Mass and, once or twice a week, Holy Communion and his thanksgiving. Then breakfast, taken in silence. He read in a spiritual book for half an hour or so after breakfast, then went to the kitchen or the dining hall or the scullery, where he set to work under the orders of the cook.

In the course of the morning there might be a talk or instruction from the priest in charge of the novices. There surely would be one or more visits to the chapel. When the hour for dinner came, Stanislaus probably served at table, taking his own meal later. After dinner there was an hour for recreation, when the novices walked and chatted in the garden or about the house.

The afternoon, like the morning, was taken up with lowly work, with prayer, and a little reading or instruction. Toward evening, he again spent half an hour in meditation. Then came the evening meal, another hour of recreation, a little reading in preparation for next morning's meditation, and examination of conscience as to how the day had been spent, and then bed.

Two or three days a week, this routine was broken. Sometimes the novices walked out into the country to a villa, where they had games and ate their dinner. At other times they left their work to go with one of the Fathers to some church or other, upon business.

It was a quiet, humble life, full of peace, near to God, hidden away from men. In this life the novices had to continue for two years, before they took upon themselves the obligation of vows, and before they began the long studies that prepare a Jesuit for his work. During those two years they tested their vocation, making sure that God really called them to that life; and they tested their own wills to see if they were ready to endure what such a life demanded of them.

Stanislaus did just what the other novices did, did nothing out of the ordinary. Yet, of course, he was different from the others; he was a saint. What was the difference? Just this: they did things more or less well; he did things perfectly. If he prayed, he put his whole mind and soul into his prayer. If he worked, he obeyed orders absolutely, because in doing so he was obeying God.

There is in the Jesuit noviciate at Angers a series of paintings portraying incidents in the life of Stanislaus. In one he is shown carrying on his arm two or three bits of wood towards the kitchen. Underneath is written, "He will err if he carry more."

The painting commemorates an occasion when Stanislaus and Claude Acquaviva were put by the cook to carry wood and told to carry only two or three pieces at a time. Acquaviva, when the two came to the wood-pile, said laughingly:

"Does the cook think we are babies? Why, we can each carry twenty or thirty of such little pieces of wood."

"To be sure we can," Stanislaus answered. "But do you think God wants us to carry twenty or thirty pieces now? The cook said two or three, and the cook just at present takes the place of God to command us."

And so it was in everything. He studied singly to see what would please God most, and no matter how trifling seemed the command he did just that, with all his heart.

No one ever heard a sharp word from him, or saw him take offense at anything, or act in the least way out of vanity or selfishness.

And, of course, he was entirely unconscious that he was different from the rest. He knew he was trying to do his best in everything, but he supposed every one else was doing the same. And with all his earnestness and exactness, he was as simple and boyish as he had ever been.

One day Cardinal Commendoni, the Legate to Vienna, and a great friend of Stanislaus, came to Rome and hurried over to the Roman College to call upon Stanislaus. Stanislaus, as soon as he heard of his arrival, ran off to meet him just as he was, sleeves rolled up, apron on, straight from the scullery - just as any boy would do.

He was in everything perfectly at ease; content in his little round of little tasks; going ahead toward heaven without any show or heroics. He was doing just exactly the little things that God wants us to do, and he was entirely happy in so doing.

It is true he had never been really unhappy in his whole life. People who keep close to God never are. They have hard things to put up with; they may be poor, or fall sick, or lose their relatives or friends by death; they may have to fight very strong temptations. They feel all these things as keenly as others feel them. But they do not become unhappy. We may say they have a world of their own to live in, that their inmost lives are spent in that world, very little touched by the changes and accidents of the outer world. They see that there is an outer world, but they choose deliberately to ignore it; they will not go into it.

You know that if you go down deep into the sea, as men go in submarines, you find calm there always, even though a storm be raging up above and the waves toss with angry violence. So if you once get inside your life, under the surface, in the heart of life where God is, you will find calm there also and a certain peace which is as near as we can come to entire happiness in this world.

But though Stanislaus had learned this secret, and had therefore always kept his soul merry, he was happiest of all during the time of his noviceship. The very air around him breathed of God and heaven. His life there was really an unbroken prayer. He was like a swimmer who has been fighting his way through nasty, choppy, little waves, going ahead surely, but with great difficulty, and who comes at last into long, quiet, rolling swells, where his progress is delightful, where he can make long, easy strokes and feel pleasure in the very effort.

And as he was young and ardent, he was in danger of overdoing things. Prayer, even when it is a joy, is always hard work for us poor mortals. Stanislaus gave himself so heartily now to praying that he ran risk of losing his strength and health. So his superiors, being sensible men, stepped in and moderated his energy. He was made to work more and pray less, told to be prudent, to husband his strength for future work. And, of course, he did as he was told.

But God had special designs on Stanislaus. He was never to use his health and energy in work as a priest or teacher. Indeed, his work was nearly over, though it had been so brief. He had no long career before him on this earth; he was going home, and going soon.

CHAPTER XIV
GOING HOME

When Stanislaus had been a novice nine months, Peter Canisius came one day to Rome on business. At this time Stanislaus was living in the noviciate proper, Sant' Andrea on the Quirinal. Of course the novices were all keen to see and hear the great Canisius, the man who had done such superb work in Germany. And whatever curiosity they had was satisfied, for Canisius came to the community at Sant' Andrea and gave a little sermon or talk.

It was the first of August, the month always most dangerous to health in Rome. Just for that reason, perhaps, the old Romans had made the beginning of that month a time of feasting and boisterous holiday. And an old proverb had come down, "Ferrare Agosto - Give August a jolly welcome"

Canisius took this proverb for his text, but turned it to say, "Give every month a jolly welcome, for it may be your last."

After the talk, the novices, according to custom, discussed amongst themselves what had been said. It came Stanislaus' turn to speak. He said:

"What Father Canisius has just told us is a holy warning for all, of course. But for me it is something more, because this month of August is to be really my last month 'upon earth."

To be sure, no one paid special attention to this strange remark. Novices often say things that will not bear too much analysis. Particularly no one would look seriously upon what Stanislaus had said, since he was at the time in perfect health.

Four days later, the feast of our Lady of the Snows, Stanislaus had occasion to go with the great theologian, Father Emmanuel de Sa, to the church of Santa Maria Maggiore. For there the beautiful feast is kept with singular ceremony, as that church is the one connected with the origin of the feast. Each year, during Vespers on August 5th, a shower of jasmin leaves sifts down from the high dome of a chapel in Santa Maria Maggiore, to commemorate the miraculous snow in August which marked out the spot where the church was to be built.

As they went along, de Sa turned the talk to the coming feast of the Assumption of our Blessed Lady. Stanislaus spoke with delight, as he always spoke of our Lady.

"When our Lady entered paradise," he said, "I think God made a new glory for His Mother, and all the saints made a court about her and did reverence to her as we do to a king. And I hope," he added; "that I shall be up there myself to enjoy this coming feast."

Again his words were not taken at their face value. Father de Sa thought he spoke of being in heaven in spirit for the feast.

The practice, now common, was new then, of alloting to each in the community as special patron some particular saint whose feast occurred during the month. Stanislaus had drawn Saint Lawrence for his patron. The feast of the Saint is celebrated on August 10th. Stanislaus, who had clear intimations of his quickly approaching death, and was eager to go to heaven, asked Saint Lawrence to intercede for him that his home-going might be on the Feast of the Assumption. He got permission to practice some penances in honor of the Saint. He prepared for the feast with unusual devotion. On the morning of the 10th when he went to Holy Communion, he carried on his breast a letter he had written to our Lady. It was such a letter as a boy, away from home, and homesick, might write to his mother, asking her to bring him home.

After breakfast, Stanislaus, still in entire health, was sent to work in the kitchen, where he spent the rest of the morning, washing dishes, carrying wood for the fire, helping the cook generally.

But by evening he was decidedly unwell. To the fellow-novice who helped him to bed he said quietly, "I am going to die, you know, in a few days."

Claude Acquaviva hurried to him as soon as he learned he was ailing. Father Fazio, the novice-master, also came. Stanislaus told each of the favor he had begged from our Lady, and that he hoped strongly his request would be granted.

That was on the evening of Wednesday, the 10th. He appeared to be no better or worse on Thursday and Friday. But Friday evening he was moved from his ordinary room to a quieter place in a higher story of the house. Those who went with him noted that before he lay down, he knelt on the floor and prayed a while and made the sign of the cross over the bed, saying, "This is my deathbed."

Now they began to believe him and were frightened a little. So Stanislaus added, with a smile, "I mean, of course, if it so please God." He continued in about the same condition until Sunday, August 14th. That day he said to the laybrother who was taking care of him:

"Brother, I'm going to die to-night."

The brother laughed at him, and said:

"Nonsense, man! Why, it would take a greater miracle to die of so trifling a matter than to be cured of it."

But by noon of that day Stanislaus became unconscious. Father Fazio was with him at once and administered restoratives. Very soon Stanislaus was himself again, bright and smiling as ever. Father Fazio began to joke with him.

"O man of little heart!" he said. "To give up courage in so slight a sickness!"

Stanislaus answered, "A man of little heart I admit I am. But the sickness, Father, is not so very slight, since I'm going to die of it."

And, indeed, he began to fail rapidly. By evening the death-sweat stood out upon him, the vital warmth little by little withdrew from hands and feet to the citadel of his heart. When the last light of day was gone from the sky, he made his confession and received the Holy Viaticum. A great many of his fellow-novices were present, and some wept. He was a good comrade, they did not want to see him depart from them.

Then he received Extreme Unction. He made the answers to the prayers himself. Afterward he confessed again, in order to receive the plenary indulgence granted for the hour of death. And after that he talked for a little time, kindly and cheerfully, to those about him, and bidding them good-by, turned his mind and his heart to heaven.

Three Fathers stayed with him through the silence of the night, when the rest had gone to bed. Most of the time he prayed, either aloud with his watchers, or silently by himself. He left messages to his more intimate friends, and asked the Fathers to beg pardon for any offense he had given.

During the evening he had begged to be laid on the bare ground, that he might die as a penitent. Toward midnight, as he still asked it, they lifted him on the little mattress of his bed and placed him on it upon the floor. There he lay, very quiet, whilst midnight tolled from the great churches of the city. The Fathers knelt beside him, praying silently with him, or giving him from time to time the crucifix to kiss.

At length, about three o'clock in the morning, he stopped praying, and a great joy shone in his face. He looked about him from side to side, and seemed with his eyes to ask his companions to join him in reverencing some one who was present.

Father Ruiz bent over and asked him:

What is it, Stanislaus?

"Our Lady!" he whispered. "Our Lady has come, just as in Vienna."

Then he seemed to listen to voices they could not hear. His lips moved silently, forming inaudible words. His eyes were bright and joyful. He stretched out his arms, fell back, and died with a smile upon his lips. Our Lady had come for him, and with her he went home. Dawn was breaking on the Feast of the Assumption, 1568.

CHAPTER XV
AFTERMATH

Stanislaus lacked six or eight weeks of being eighteen years old when he died. He had not been a preacher or writer or engaged in any public work. Only a handful of people in Rome so much as knew of his existence. Yet no sooner was he dead than crowds flocked about him as about a dead saint.

The General, Francis Borgia, ordered the body to be put into a coffin, which was an unusual thing at that time, and to be buried at the right hand of the high altar in the church.

Meantime the Lord John Kostka still raged in Poland. He had written a most severe letter to Stanislaus shortly after Stanislaus arrived in Rome: a letter full of threats and anger, to which Stanislaus had replied kindly and affectionately, explaining to his father that he had to follow God's call at any cost

But the Lord John was not to be so easily put off. He ordered his eldest son, Paul, on to Rome, with power to bring back Stanislaus to his home at Kostkov.

Paul traveled in some state and with no great haste. He reached Rome in the middle of September, 1568, to find that God had been beforehand with him, and that Stanislaus had indeed already gone home, to heaven.

He had been greatly impressed at the time of Stanislaus' flight from Vienna, by the incidents which seemed to show God's direct guidance and protection in regard to his brother. Now, when the Fathers led him to the still new tomb of Stanislaus, he broke down utterly and cried like a child. He stayed a time beside the tomb, and when he came forth he was a different Paul.

Every one was talking with admiration of Stanislaus and of the marvels that had surrounded his life and death. Paul hurried back to Poland with his story, at once sad and joyful. The heart of the old Castellan was moved. He had lost a son, but he had gained a saint.

A year later appeared two short Lives of Stanislaus, one in Polish by Father Warscewiski, his fellow-novice, another in Latin. All through Poland the devotion to the young novice spread rapidly. Soon authoritative "processes" toward his beatification were drawn up under the care of the bishops of various places in which Stanislaus had spent his short years.

Thirty-six years after his death, Pope Clement VIII issued a brief (February 18, 1604) in which he declared Stanislaus "Blessed" and granted indulgences on the anniversary of his death.

But long before this the Lord John had died, and his youngest son, Albert, struck by sudden congestion of the lungs before his father's body was laid to rest, died also, and was buried in the same grave with him.

Of the four sons only Paul was left. From the day he stood by the tomb of Stanislaus, he had changed entirely. Bitter remembrance of his harshness and brutality to the dead saint was with him always and urged him to a life of penance and prayer. He never married, but passed his days largely at the castle of Kostkov in retirement with his widowed mother.

He busied himself in constant works of charity, spending his great fortune in helping the poor and in establishing hospitals and building churches. He wore himself out in prayer and labor and fasting. Men marveled at him, and many sneered at him, as he had once sneered at Stanislaus.

But those long, hard years were not unhappy for him. He and his mother, Margaret Kostka, had learned Stanislaus' secret of happiness, and lived in spirit in that bright home to which Stanislaus had gone.

Then Margaret died, and Paul was alone. He had wished to withdraw from the world altogether. But he felt unworthy to ask admission into a religious order. However, realizing at length that his death could not be far distant, and that he could at worst be a burden for only a very short time, he wrote to Claude Acquaviva, who was then General of the Society of Jesus, and begged that he might at least die in the Society to which Stanislaus had belonged. Acquaviva readily dispensed with the impediment of age and ordered the Provincial of Poland, Father Strinieno, to receive him.

Paul hastened to the royal court, then at Pietscop, to settle his worldly affairs before taking up his residence in the noviceship. But scarcely had he completed his arrangements, when fever seized him, and he died after a few days' illness. He died November 13, 1607: the very day of the month afterwards fixed as the feast of Saint Stanislaus.

Bilinski, too, the tutor of Stanislaus, showed in after life the fruit of Stanislaus' prayers. He became Canon of Pultowa and Plock and lived holily. It was his privilege to bear testimony to many events in the life of Stanislaus, and he was a very valuable witness in the "processes" for his pupil's beatification. When death came, Stanislaus appeared to him in vision, consoling and encouraging him, and he died in great peace.

All this time the people of Poland had been eager in their devotion to the Blessed Stanislaus. Many cures and miracles had been wrought through his intercession. In 1621, under the Polish king, Sigismund III, and again in 1676, under Yan Sobieski, the Poles won pronounced victories over Turkish armies which far outnumbered their own, and attributed these preternatural successes to the prayers of Stanislaus.

The whole nation, through its kings, repeatedly petitioned that Stanislaus might be declared their Patron. This was at first refused, as only canonized saints were given the title of Patron of a nation. But Clement x granted the request in 1671, setting aside the decree which forbade it.

The Church is slow in declaring any one a saint. It was not until December 13, 1726, one hundred and fifty-eight years after the death of Stanislaus, that Benedict XIII solemnly celebrated his canonization in the Basilica of St. Peter. It was a double ceremony, for it was also the occasion of the canonization of Saint Aloysius, who had been born in March of the same year in which Stanislaus died.

This little account has not done justice to the life of Stanislaus Kostka; and, indeed, it is very hard to do justice to it. He was a most human and lovable boy, but he was besides a wonderful, bright being that eludes the grip of our common minds. He was a citizen of heaven, who lived here amongst us, kindly and companionable indeed, during eighteen years of exile. To try to describe him is like trying to describe a star in the far sky of night.

That love for God, of which we speak so brokenly, which at its best in us is so small and cold, was the soul of his soul, the inner core and substance of his life.

Here, in the misty country of faith, he had something of that radiant and rapturous union with God which all of us, as we hope, shall one day have in heaven.

All the sweet and strong twining of our hearts about father and mother and relatives and dear friends, all that binds us in affection to those we love in life, was multiplied and made many times stronger in his rare nature and lifted up by God's grace to fix itself upon God, the infinite Goodness, the supreme Beauty.

God was not a mere Name or a Power to him, not even the mere Lord and Master of all: God was his friend, his dearest intimate, his sure, strong, patient, loving counselor; whose presence was with him, waking and sleeping; whose interests were nearest his heart; whose commands it was a delight to obey; whose slightest wish and beckoning was eagerly watched for and joyously followed.

To catch the secret and true meaning of his life, one must feel how that love for God thrilled through him, was his. courage in action, his endurance in suffering, his sweetness and kindness in all dealings with other men. It was his life. And when we have said and realized that, we have come nearest to knowing who and what really was Stanislaus Kostka.

The Codes Of Hammurabi And Moses
W. W. Davies

The discovery of the Hammurabi Code is one of the greatest achievements of archaeology, and is of paramount interest, not only to the student of the Bible, but also to all those interested in ancient history...

Religion   ISBN: *1-59462-338-4*

QTY

Pages:132

MSRP $12.95

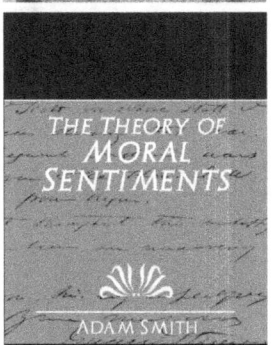

The Theory of Moral Sentiments
Adam Smith

This work from 1749. contains original theories of conscience amd moral judgment and it is the foundation for systemof morals.

Philosophy ISBN: *1-59462-777-0*

QTY

Pages:536

MSRP $19.95

Jessica's First Prayer
Hesba Stretton

QTY

In a screened and secluded corner of one of the many railway-bridges which span the streets of London there could be seen a few years ago, from five o'clock every morning until half past eight, a tidily set-out coffee-stall, consisting of a trestle and board, upon which stood two large tin cans, with a small fire of charcoal burning under each so as to keep the coffee boiling during the early hours of the morning when the work-people were thronging into the city on their way to their daily toil...

Childrens   ISBN: *1-59462-373-2*

Pages:84

MSRP $9.95

My Life and Work
Henry Ford

QTY

Henry Ford revolutionized the world with his implementation of mass production for the Model T automobile. Gain valuable business insight into his life and work with his own auto-biography... "We have only started on our development of our country we have not as yet, with all our talk of wonderful progress, done more than scratch the surface. The progress has been wonderful enough but..."

Biographies/   ISBN: *1-59462-198-5*

Pages:300

MSRP $21.95

www.bookjungle.com *email: sales@bookjungle.com fax: 630-214-0564 mail: Book Jungle PO Box 2226 Champaign, IL 61825*

The Art of Cross-Examination
Francis Wellman

QTY

I presume it is the experience of every author, after his first book is published upon an important subject, to be almost overwhelmed with a wealth of ideas and illustrations which could readily have been included in his book, and which to his own mind, at least, seem to make a second edition inevitable. Such certainly was the case with me; and when the first edition had reached its sixth impression in five months, I rejoiced to learn that it seemed to my publishers that the book had met with a sufficiently favorable reception to justify a second and considerably enlarged edition. ..

Pages:412

Reference   **ISBN: *1-59462-647-2***   *MSRP $19.95*

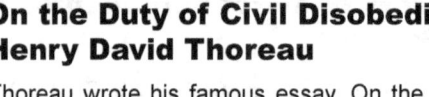

On the Duty of Civil Disobedience
Henry David Thoreau

QTY

Thoreau wrote his famous essay, On the Duty of Civil Disobedience, as a protest against an unjust but popular war and the immoral but popular institution of slave-owning. He did more than write—he declined to pay his taxes, and was hauled off to gaol in consequence. Who can say how much this refusal of his hastened the end of the war and of slavery ?

Law   **ISBN: *1-59462-747-9***   **Pages:48**

MSRP $7.45

Dream Psychology Psychoanalysis for Beginners
Sigmund Freud

QTY

Sigmund Freud, born Sigismund Schlomo Freud (May 6, 1856 - September 23, 1939), was a Jewish-Austrian neurologist and psychiatrist who co-founded the psychoanalytic school of psychology. Freud is best known for his theories of the unconscious mind, especially involving the mechanism of repression; his redefinition of sexual desire as mobile and directed towards a wide variety of objects; and his therapeutic techniques, especially his understanding of transference in the therapeutic relationship and the presumed value of dreams as sources of insight into unconscious desires.

Pages:196

Psychology   **ISBN: *1-59462-905-6***   *MSRP $15.45*

The Miracle of Right Thought
Orison Swett Marden

QTY

Believe with all of your heart that you will do what you were made to do. When the mind has once formed the habit of holding cheerful, happy, prosperous pictures, it will not be easy to form the opposite habit. It does not matter how improbable or how far away this realization may see, or how dark the prospects may be, if we visualize them as best we can, as vividly as possible, hold tenaciously to them and vigorously struggle to attain them, they will gradually become actualized, realized in the life. But a desire, a longing without endeavor, a yearning abandoned or held indifferently will vanish without realization.

Pages:360

Self Help   **ISBN: *1-59462-644-8***   *MSRP $25.45*

QTY

The Rosicrucian Cosmo-Conception Mystic Christianity *by Max Heindel*   ISBN: *1-59462-188-8* **$38.95**
The Rosicrucian Cosmo-conception is not dogmatic, neither does it appeal to any other authority than the reason of the student. It is: not controversial, but is; sent forth in the, hope that it may help to clear...   New Age/Religion Pages 646

Abandonment To Divine Providence *by Jean-Pierre de Caussade*   ISBN: *1-59462-228-0* **$25.95**
"The Rev. Jean Pierre de Caussade was one of the most remarkable spiritual writers of the Society of Jesus in France in the 18th Century. His death took place at Toulouse in 1751. His works have gone through many editions and have been republished...   Inspirational/Religion Pages 400

Mental Chemistry *by Charles Haanel*   ISBN: *1-59462-192-6* **$23.95**
Mental Chemistry allows the change of material conditions by combining and appropriately utilizing the power of the mind. Much like applied chemistry creates something new and unique out of careful combinations of chemicals the mastery of mental chemistry...   New Age Pages 354

The Letters of Robert Browning and Elizabeth Barret Barrett 1845-1846 vol II   ISBN: *1-59462-193-4* **$35.95**
by Robert Browning and Elizabeth Barrett   Biographies Pages 596

Gleanings In Genesis (volume I) *by Arthur W. Pink*   ISBN: *1-59462-130-6* **$27.45**
Appropriately has Genesis been termed "the seed plot of the Bible" for in it we have, in germ form, almost all of the great doctrines which are afterwards fully developed in the books of Scripture which follow...   Religion/Inspirational Pages 420

The Master Key *by L. W. de Laurence*   ISBN: *1-59462-001-6* **$30.95**
In no branch of human knowledge has there been a more lively increase of the spirit of research during the past few years than in the study of Psychology, Concentration and Mental Discipline. The requests for authentic lessons in Thought Control, Mental Discipline and...   New Age/Business Pages 422

The Lesser Key Of Solomon Goetia *by L. W. de Laurence*   ISBN: *1-59462-092-X* **$9.95**
This translation of the first book of the "Lernegton" which is now for the first time made accessible to students of Talismanic Magic was done, after careful collation and edition, from numerous Ancient Manuscripts in Hebrew, Latin, and French...   New Age/Occult Pages 92

Rubaiyat Of Omar Khayyam *by Edward Fitzgerald*   ISBN:*1-59462-332-5* **$13.95**
Edward Fitzgerald, whom the world has already learned, in spite of his own efforts to remain within the shadow of anonymity, to look upon as one of the rarest poets of the century, was born at Bredfield, in Suffolk, on the 31st of March, 1809. He was the third son of John Purcell...   Music Pages 172

Ancient Law *by Henry Maine*   ISBN: *1-59462-128-4* **$29.95**
The chief object of the following pages is to indicate some of the earliest ideas of mankind, as they are reflected in Ancient Law, and to point out the relation of those ideas to modern thought.   Religiom/History Pages 452

Far-Away Stories *by William J. Locke*   ISBN: *1-59462-129-2* **$19.45**
"Good wine needs no bush, but a collection of mixed vintages does. And this book is just such a collection. Some of the stories I do not want to remain buried for ever in the museum files of dead magazine-numbers an author's not unpardonable vanity..."   Fiction Pages 272

Life of David Crockett *by David Crockett*   ISBN: *1-59462-250-7* **$27.45**
"Colonel David Crockett was one of the most remarkable men of the times in which he lived. Born in humble life, but gifted with a strong will, an indomitable courage, and unremitting perseverance...   Biographies/New Age Pages 424

Lip-Reading *by Edward Nitchie*   ISBN: *1-59462-206-X* **$25.95**
Edward B. Nitchie, founder of the New York School for the Hard of Hearing, now the Nitchie School of Lip-Reading, Inc, wrote "LIP-READING Principles and Practice". The development and perfecting of this meritorious work on lip-reading was an undertaking...   How-to Pages 400

A Handbook of Suggestive Therapeutics, Applied Hypnotism, Psychic Science   ISBN: *1-59462-214-0* **$24.95**
by Henry Munro   Health/New Age/Health/Self-help Pages 376

A Doll's House: and Two Other Plays *by Henrik Ibsen*   ISBN: *1-59462-112-8* **$19.95**
Henrik Ibsen created this classic when in revolutionary 1848 Rome. Introducing some striking concepts in playwriting for the realist genre, this play has been studied the world over.   Fiction/Classics/Plays 308

The Light of Asia *by sir Edwin Arnold*   ISBN: *1-59462-204-3* **$13.95**
In this poetic masterpiece, Edwin Arnold describes the life and teachings of Buddha. The man who was to become known as Buddha to the world was born as Prince Gautama of India but he rejected the worldly riches and abandoned the reigns of power when...   Religion/History/Biographies Pages 170

The Complete Works of Guy de Maupassant *by Guy de Maupassant*   ISBN: *1-59462-157-8* **$16.95**
"For days and days, nights and nights, I had dreamed of that first kiss which was to consecrate our engagement, and I knew not on what spot I should put my lips..."   Fiction/Classics Pages 240

The Art of Cross-Examination *by Francis L. Wellman*   ISBN: *1-59462-309-0* **$26.95**
Written by a renowned trial lawyer, Wellman imparts his experience and uses case studies to explain how to use psychology to extract desired information through questioning.   How-to/Science/Reference Pages 408

Answered or Unanswered? *by Louisa Vaughan*   ISBN: *1-59462-248-5* **$10.95**
Miracles of Faith in China   Religion Pages 112

The Edinburgh Lectures on Mental Science (1909) *by Thomas*   ISBN: *1-59462-008-3* **$11.95**
This book contains the substance of a course of lectures recently given by the writer in the Queen Street Hall, Edinburgh. Its purpose is to indicate the Natural Principles governing the relation between Mental Action and Material Conditions...   New Age/Psychology Pages 148

Ayesha *by H. Rider Haggard*   ISBN: *1-59462-301-5* **$24.95**
Verily and indeed it is the unexpected that happens! Probably if there was one person upon the earth from whom the Editor of this, and of a certain previous history, did not expect to hear again...   Classics Pages 380

Ayala's Angel *by Anthony Trollope*   ISBN: *1-59462-352-X* **$29.95**
The two girls were both pretty, but Lucy who was twenty-one who supposed to be simple and comparatively unattractive, whereas Ayala was credited, as her Bombwhat romantic name might show, with poetic charm and a taste for romance. Ayala when her father died was nineteen...   Fiction Pages 484

The American Commonwealth *by James Bryce*   ISBN: *1-59462-286-8* **$34.45**
An interpretation of American democratic political theory. It examines political mechanics and society from the perspective of Scotsman James Bryce   Politics Pages 572

Stories of the Pilgrims *by Margaret P. Pumphrey*   ISBN: *1-59462-116-0* **$17.95**
This book explores pilgrims religious oppression in England as well as their escape to Holland and eventual crossing to America on the Mayflower, and their early days in New England...   History Pages 268

QTY

The Fasting Cure *by Sinclair Upton*   ISBN: *1-59462-222-1*   **$13.95**
In the Cosmopolitan Magazine for May, 1910, and in the Contemporary Review (London) for April, 1910, I published an article dealing with my experiences in fasting. I have written a great many magazine articles, but never one which attracted so much attention... New Age/Self Help/Health Pages 164

Hebrew Astrology *by Sepharial*   ISBN: *1-59462-308-2*   **$13.45**
In these days of advanced thinking it is a matter of common observation that we have left many of the old landmarks behind and that we are now pressing forward to greater heights and to a wider horizon than that which represented the mind-content of our progenitors... Astrology Pages 144

Thought Vibration or The Law of Attraction in the Thought World   ISBN: *1-59462-127-6*   **$12.95**
by William Walker Atkinson   *Psychology/Religion Pages 144*

Optimism *by Helen Keller*   ISBN: *1-59462-108-X*   **$15.95**
Helen Keller was blind, deaf, and mute since 19 months old, yet famously learned how to overcome these handicaps, communicate with the world, and spread her lectures promoting optimism. An inspiring read for everyone... Biographies/Inspirational Pages 84

Sara Crewe *by Frances Burnett*   ISBN: *1-59462-360-0*   **$9.45**
In the first place, Miss Minchin lived in London. Her home was a large, dull, tall one, in a large, dull square, where all the houses were alike, and all the sparrows were alike, and where all the door-knockers made the same heavy sound... Childrens/Classic Pages 88

The Autobiography of Benjamin Franklin *by Benjamin Franklin*   ISBN: *1-59462-135-7*   **$24.95**
The Autobiography of Benjamin Franklin has probably been more extensively read than any other American historical work, and no other book of its kind has had such ups and downs of fortune. Franklin lived for many years in England, where he was agent... Biographies/History Pages 332

Name	
Email	
Telephone	
Address	
City, State ZIP	

☐ **Credit Card**   ☐ **Check / Money Order**

Credit Card Number	
Expiration Date	
Signature	

Please Mail to: Book Jungle
PO Box 2226
Champaign, IL 61825
or Fax to: 630-214-0564

ORDERING INFORMATION

web*: www.bookjungle.com*
email*: sales@bookjungle.com*
fax*: 630-214-0564*
mail*: Book Jungle PO Box 2226 Champaign, IL 61825*
or PayPal *to sales@bookjungle.com*

Please contact us for bulk discounts

DIRECT-ORDER TERMS

**20% Discount if You Order
Two or More Books**
Free Domestic Shipping!
Accepted: Master Card, Visa,
Discover, American Express

www.ingramcontent.com/pod-product-compliance
Lightning Source LLC
Chambersburg PA
CBHW080749250626
47162CB00010B/3072